ANY OTHER *FUNNY* BUSINESS

Mike Fitzsimons

Thanks to my wife Michelle without whose encouragement and help this book would not have been written.

Thanks also to the Maire and all the local people for their kindness and welcome to their wonderful community.

CONTENTS

CHAPTER 1

THE MEETING BEFORE THE FIRST MEETING

Before the brief speeches by each person in turn had worked even half their way around the group I had decided that the language was incomprehensible, and I was paying the barest minimum of attention to the words spoken. My mind was switching back and forth between THAT telephone conversation three weeks earlier and the conversation I would have later that night at home explaining to my wife why it would be impossible for me to continue.

♦ ♦ ♦

'No way!' I had said.

'Oh dear,' she had replied, 'that's a shame. Why not?'

My poor comprehension of the language, and my unfamiliarity with everything French, not to mention the peculiarities of the

French voting system, had left me in no doubt that there must be someone in the commune more eligible than me.

'Well the language for a start. My French is terrible, and I wouldn't want to support everything just for the British.'

'Oh, go on it would be really good for your French and help us to integrate. It will be interesting.'

I noted the change of tense. Conditional/future. This wouldn't have meant anything 12 months earlier.

I was flattered, of course, who wouldn't have been, by a visit from the neighbour to introduce the Maire? A *deputation* as my wife called it when she eagerly telephoned me in the UK where I was on one of my flying visits to see the kids again (trying to keep my promise of monthly visits since our move to south-west France some 18 months earlier).

Appealing to my ego was a smart move on her part. Having not long arrived in France from England, she knew I was hardly likely to turn down the offer to be a local councillor!

So, three weeks after I said I would think about it I received the summons, not to the Mairie where council meetings would normally be held, but to the *commune* community hall, where the tables had been arranged in the form of a large rectangle at one end of the hall. We did not really need all these tables, since there were only 11 of us but with Madame le Maire occupying the whole of one side (no doubt to give her more authority) I wondered if the others also felt like school children who had been helping teacher and were now to get their reward as class monitor.

Some who were a little too eager were gently being put down a peg or two by Madame le Maire, and those who were a little reticent, having been hooked, were now being drawn in on her line.

She was only to be Madame le Maire for a few more days, up until the local election. This period was a strange hiatus when, judging by the importance given to it, you almost expected to see people wondering about aimlessly without the direction and guidance of the all-powerful Madame le Maire.

I looked at the 10 people sitting around the table plus the Maire at the head. I was not surprised that I had no idea what she said, as she spoke French fast with a strong local accent. I worked out that one by one people were introducing themselves with a brief history that they thought was relevant and of interest to the other potential representatives for the local *commune* council.

As the incomprehensible introductions drew closer to me, and I tried to think how I could join up the couple of dozen words I knew that might be relevant, I remembered a scene in a Bob Hope film where his ego has allowed him to be appointed Sheriff of a town and he is facing a shootout in a few minutes. He walks down the main street mindlessly repeating under his breath instructions he has been given by well-meaning townsfolk – 'He crouches when he shoots so lean to the left... The wind's from the east so stand on your toes ...,' and so on.

Having retired just before we moved to France I had seen this invitation to join the council as a new vocation, ignoring the fact that there were only one hundred and twenty four residents in the *commune*, and allowing for those who were too young to stand, too old to stand (literally), and to avoid having two people from one family on the committee, what it boils down to, allowing for two or three who had said 'no' before me, and those with whom the Maire's family had apparently had a feud some time in the last 200 years, is that I was one of the last people who might be considered eligible. The helpful advice I had received floated across my mind, and I repeated it in Bob Hope fashion. 'Just be yourself, take deep smiles, breathe at them, relax your eyes, look into their hands...'

There was an embarrassed silence when I finished what even I thought was unintelligible gibberish and having realised by the length of my pause that I had in fact stopped, Madame le Maire kindly thanked me (at least I think that's what she did) and moved on to the next.

I have said that there were 10 councillors, but in fact there were only nine present. I was later to understand that the tenth, by the name of Frédèric, was regrettably unable to be there that night because although his name was on the list, by virtue of the fact that his mother had a house in the *commune*, he worked in Paris. Nevertheless, he seemed well-known to all and it was understood that he would go along with everything we said.

For now, the introductions finished, the Maire waved about some papers in her hand.

Madame le Maire was, as I was to discover later, fond of what amounted at first hearing to a curious *shorthand* way of speaking, often used in conjunction with a sort of sign language. This would generally take the form of an expression of her point of view in normal joined-up words on the point at issue, and when she eventually stopped speaking or when someone else managed to speak louder, she would listen for a minute or two and then the shorthand sound would come out of her mouth.

Perhaps 'A!'. This is not this is not the long 'Ahh!' of comprehension, but a brusque, short, sharp expression of the 'a 'vowel as in the word 'cat'. What it actually meant was, 'Notwithstanding the point of view that I have just expressed with all my conviction, now I have heard what you have to say I'm inclined to think that what I said was possibly open to some slight question and I am minded to consider more fully what you are saying.'

If this was accompanied by a drawing of the two sides of her cardigan across her bosom slowly, it meant she probably meant what she had *previously* expressed. But beware the quick drawing of the cardigan across the bosom, for this indicated a possible sitting on the fence for a while until something more positive came along.

The 'A!' sound was not to be confused with 'Ahah,' an elongated version of the previous exclamation, which was reserved for instances where it was clear to everyone including Madame le Maire that she had been barking loudly up the wrong tree, but that of course it was not her fault – far from it - and the other contributor was a blithering idiot for only a partial release of vital information, 'without which I don't know how I could possibly be expected to have grasped a full understanding of the problem and come up with a sensible solution'. It carried with it the implication of information deliberately withheld to make her look an idiot. If accompanied by the closure of the cardi, this spelt great danger for the other contributor, who might be volunteered at the next opportunity to attend an obscure meeting in an obscure place round the back of somewhere more obscure to represent the *commune* in matters something to do with something with an obscure confusing acronym about something equally obscure reporting back to Madame le Maire in full detail. Or else.

The sort of response feared by many was the verbal command '*Attends!*', which in effect meant 'Think very carefully before you say any more in that vein.' Or, even worse, '*Écoutes!*' which really means, 'I will not put up with this, and you'd better think very carefully about your future before you say more.'

Any of these expressions accompanied by a drawing of the cardi meant almost certainly a short measure of sparkling wine at the meeting's end, and only a thin slice of cake.

Another common expression was '*Bon'*, which could mean 'good', but perhaps was a way of hedging her bets and might also mean 'Not too bad - so far - but tread carefully.'

It was sensible at this point to look out for any movement of the cardi which may give some indication of which way the wind was blowing.

In any case most of the above would be employed from the moment I started speaking, together with a squinting of the eyes and a tilting of the head as if this would improve her ability to understand my very poor French. If the mouth was screwed up as well, I knew that I was completely wasting my time.

A shuffling of the papers in front of her or rearranging them in no particular order and then banging them down on the desk, meant, 'We're coming to the end of this conversation and I don't wish to hear much more on the subject.'

At this our introductory meeting, this was all still to learn, and for now the paper in Madame le Maire 's hand was then passed around the table. I had no idea what it was initially, and it was several minutes before I guessed that it was a draft manifesto which would be made available to members of the *commune* who were eligible to vote.

My wife had been assured that the whole exercise was entirely non-political, so as I was intrigued what the manifesto might say. I have no idea to this day what it did say, but there was a series of paragraphs presumably conveying a hint of what we stood for, whatever that was. However, I noticed that each paragraph started with the word '*Nous*' ('we'). *We* would do this, and *we* would do that.

Now I hadn't been in marketing, but my business activity brought me in very close contact with it, so after waiting for a suitable pause in the animated discussion around the table, which I hoped signalled the end of one discussion and a brief interlude before the next, I weighed in.

I should have realised immediately that this was a terrible mistake. I soon did so, when for the second time that evening I saw the Maire's tilted facial expression with the added jeopardy of one hand close to the cardi in readiness. When I had stopped, and no one said anything, I realised that no one had understood what I was saying, and the phrase 'Beam me up Scotty' came to mind.

The gist of what I had tried to say was basic marketing philosophy. You don't talk about what '*we* will do', you talk about the benefits to the customer, what '*you* will get'. Sell the sizzle not the sausage. However, the concept of sizzling sausages in relation to a political manifesto would be difficult to explain to an audience of ageing rural Frenchmen and women even if I was fluent in French.

Perhaps through confidence, naivety, or pig-headedness, because I thought that what I was saying was right, though perhaps I wasn't saying it right, and even though I could see the blank faces all around me, I just kept on digging the hole deeper instead of just shutting up or doing a runner. Rather late in the day I opted to stop digging.

I have no idea whether anyone did understand what I had said, or if they did whether they agreed or not. Most likely they had understood as much as I had of them, about zero, and the subject carried on to the next contributor while I squirmed in my seat and wondered what was holding up Scotty.

It appears I need not have worried about the election too much because as I was later to discover there was no one standing in opposition to the Maire's candidacy! However, due to the unique French voting system, this still did not necessarily mean it was a foregone conclusion. For example, had any of the 11 of us received less than 50% of the votes cast, despite there being no opposition, we should have had to go through to a second round. Nevertheless, from what I could understand only one vote was required at this second stage to secure victory.

The full details of the French electoral voting system are fully understood by very few people. However, a procedure, the fairness of which can be argued over afterwards, is generally adopted, and arguments are apparently the main point of life anyway. Thus, the election is there to provide an opportunity for social interaction.

As soon as the meeting ended I was gathering up my pencils and preparing to go home and tell my wife that it was all a big mistake, I had had enough and couldn't possibly consider carrying on. Then a couple of people, recognising that it was quite late, and all this social interaction was thirsty work, brought out from nowhere some cakes and some sparkling wine to wash them down. I thought it may have been someone's birthday.

An hour or so later I arrived home. My wife was in bed. She told me that she had waited up, eager to hear my first thoughts, but it was now late, and she was tired and drowsy. I explained with gusto and while practising gesticulations in the mirror that it hadn't been so bad once the introductions were out of the way. I explained that I put them right on some basic marketing points and generally seemed to receive the acceptance of my new friends, but when I turned to her for a response, she was fast asleep.

CHAPTER 2

THE FIRST MEETING

I looked around with due reverence at the room in the Mairie. The hub, where all power rested to ensure the smooth running of the *commune*. The building was constructed as the *commune* school with two classrooms. The Mairie had originally occupied a small room at the rear of the school but had been moved into one of the two classrooms when the school was closed in the 1970s. Small rural schools like this one continue to close down all over France as school buses come into being so that children can all be bussed into bigger towns, and as the local population declines.

Behind Madame le Maire's seat in the meeting room at the Mairie, high on the wall hung an imposing picture of the French President. The long table at which Madame le Maire sat on one side, not quite centrally, was covered in green baize which created a formal and slightly sombre atmosphere. The chairs around the table by contrast were very ordinary. Some cheap plastic stacking chairs, folding wooden ones, and two 1950s domestic, slightly wobbly, dining chairs. All of them had seen better days. None of them had arms, other of course than Madame le Maire's.

Behind us, high on the wall facing the president, rested a quite ordinary domestic plastic clock, with a solemn tick that seemed appropriate to the surroundings.

Beneath the clock were fixed several frames containing school photographs, with the youngest sitting cross-legged at the front, the next year kneeling and the next standing behind them. I was sure from looking at them earlier that six of the smallest children in one of the photographs were now sitting around the table and on later checking the date, it *was* taken about 53 years ago, which seemed about right.

Occupying a large area in one corner of the room was what appeared at first glance to be an imposing wardrobe. A curtain along part of one side made it look more like a cross between a modern photo booth and an old confessional. Perhaps a public urinal had been brought in here for safe keeping, I thought. It was of course the voting booth, which grandly came into its own only once every few years, but which waited earnestly meantime like a well-oiled guillotine for the moment when its services would be called upon, some heads would roll, and others would take up matters of state.

An ancient headmaster's desk occupied another corner of the room and I had a sudden disturbing image of Madame le Maire complete with mortar board, gown and cane ready to enforce order should that be needed.

Finally, in the last corner of the room stood a large blackboard; no doubt a relic of the previous use of the building and presumably too large to have been taken out through the door.

There I sat, slightly quivering. Trying to look both at ease and attentive. I was dressed in the formally-casual or casually-formal clothes that I had considered and rejected and considered again several times before leaving the house.

There was much laughter and many congratulations as Jean-Luc, the big chap with a very strong local accent and who was almost deaf, came in carrying 11 bottles of wine, each bearing a special label he had made up with our 11 names on it.

He hadn't quite spelled my name correctly, but it did reflect the way they pronounced it and I was quite used to any number of mis-spellings of my name by this time. The thought was there.

The meeting eventually started with apologies for absence.

Only one of the 11 was unable to be there. This was Frédèric, because apparently he had urgent business in Paris where he worked most of the time.

The remaining 10 got down to work. At least nine did whilst I looked on in helpless anxiety. When I guessed that points of view were required I tried to avoid eye contact and put on a stupid grin which varied in meaning between 'Oh yes... well possibly,' and 'Probably not', depending upon how I judged the general mood of the others.

I had long since given up any idea of trying to understand even what the subject was, never mind what had been said. Not just because of the language but also the strong local accent and speed of delivery. They didn't speak like this on my French Language CDs. Instead, I concentrated on whether there seemed to be a general mood of agreement or disagreement with whatever it was they were discussing.

This is not as easy as you might think. A topic raised by Madame le Maire could within a few minutes have two people raising their voices at each other, shouting and gesticulating. However, it was quite likely that I had completely misjudged the situation, and I learnt that it was quite possible that they were in fact in total agreement and simply trying to outdo the other in expressions of solidarity.

If one conversation at a time per subject was all that there was to contend with, it may not have been too difficult to pick up the odd word here and there. However, a little group of three women councillors occupied one corner of the long table, and the group were engrossed for almost all the evening in conversations of their own, not paying any regard to Madame le Maire or any other councillors.

The state of my mind and body was in total alert mode the entire time, simply judging whether I was being asked a question that required a response. I could often identify a question because of the raised eyebrows that accompanied an inflection in the voice.

I had to stop saying that I didn't understand the question because it would have looked as if I didn't understand *any* French, so I developed a noncommittal sort of grunt, and using the same eyebrow technique, managed to confound my questioner who was now on an equal footing, having little idea what I was asking. This certainly slowed down the enquiries directed my way.

Before coming to the meeting, I had practised a few little expressions or phrases which I hoped might be useful and probably would have been had I understood what on earth they were talking about.

Fortunately, the need to vote after discussion on any item was regarded as superfluous with Madame le Maire noting agreement or disagreement with the proposal on the table, and it was necessary to wait until the Minutes of the next meeting to discover which way the Maire decided the meeting had voted.

I couldn't wait to get away and explain to my wife that I was completely out of my depth, I just couldn't go on and we would have to find some excuse.

At the end of the meeting the sparkling wine came out, accompanied by cakes because with 11 people it was always someone's birthday just gone or just coming. Everything became much more relaxed and after the sparkling wine and cake had been consumed and someone told the three ladies at the corner of the table that we were leaving, the meeting packed up.

My wife drowsily asked how it went and was it as bad as I thought.

'Oh, I made my views known on a few complicated issues,' I found myself saying, 'and we made one or two important decisions. Well I think we did. Overall, I think I got away with it.'

'I knew you could do it,' she said, before falling asleep

CHAPTER 3

THE BUDGET

The next meeting had a different feel right from the start. First, before opening the door I could hear a dog yapping. On opening the door, I found that almost everyone had already arrived except Frédèric who worked in Paris and who I later discovered had some urgent business that evening and would be unable to come to our meeting.

Scrutinising the agenda which had arrived a few days earlier, I had noticed that in between all the standard wording about when and where the meeting was, and what to do if you couldn't come and so on, was buried the word 'Budget'.

On the large blackboard just behind Madame le Maire were written several rows and columns of figures and percentages, but I couldn't work out what they related to.

Madame le Maire was surrounded by piles of files, envelopes, books, and bits of paper, piled so high so that we could only just make out above them her hair, eyes and part of her nose, which seemed to be resting on the file that was perched precariously on top of this pile. Surrounded by the wall of paper, and with her mouth invisible to observers, her voice appeared slightly deeper and more echoey than normal, which gave her slightly more gravitas (as though she needed it!), and I wondered if this was the real purpose of the wall.

The dog in the meantime was racing around between one pair of legs and another under the table yapping away from time to time, but no one seemed to be bothered and I began to wonder if I was imagining it.

Whilst we are waiting for the meeting to start (or perhaps it had started but I was just unaware of it) Dirk the nice Dutchman lent over to me and confided, ‘You know Mike, I have been appointed a member of the finance committee.’ This was apparently a small group who usually had a meeting with Madame le Maire a few days before the budget meeting and decided everything in advance. Dirk, for whom I had acquired much respect, was after all an accountant. Strangely however, he had not received an invitation to attend such a planning meeting, and we looked at each other with growing and knowing suspicion.

As far as I could tell skipping apologies for absence and approval of the previous Minutes altogether, Madame le Maire embarked (with her eyes and half a nose visible above the pile) on an exercise that would send babies to sleep. That is, reading line after line of expenses (or were they incomes?) complete with the amounts for each one - and not just in euros, but down to the last centime.

At first I wondered if it was a joke, because I could not understand why she didn't just give us a copy of the papers she was reading from. When I say papers, I presume they were papers because all was hidden behind the wall in front of her.

The Maire’s reading went on for about 25 minutes, with her pausing only twice to pour water from a beaker to somewhere in the region of about 5 cm below the top of the files where I guessed her mouth might be.

During the 25 minutes monologue I quickly gave up trying to work out the number of euros for each item. This is partly because translating numbers is difficult enough, but in French it's even more tricky where 70 and 90 are concerned. 70 isn't too bad, though it doesn't have its own number – you must add together 60 plus 14 to get to 74 for example. But when it comes to anything above 79, multiplication and addition may be required for one number. For example, 80 does not have its own number, it is quatre-vingts - that is, 4 x 20. They make 90 not a completely new word but quatre-vingt-dix, that is 4 x 20 + 10 and so on. So that on hearing *quatre-vingt....* you multiply 4 by 20 and write down the first figure of a number that you quite logically think must begin with 8, only to have to cross it out and change it to ninety-something as soon as you hear a figure above 10 which you then add to the 4 x 20.

If this sounds complicated that's because it is. And I haven't even mentioned that whereas all the numbers ending in 1 – i.e. 21, 31 and so on have the French for 'and' between the first digit and the second – e.g. vingt *et* un. Just when you get the hang of this, you find that this system does not apply to 81 or 91. On the odd occasion when the number was easy, and I thought I had just got it, Madame le Maire added 95 centimes to the end and I completely forgot the first bit.

In any case since I had also after a few minutes given up trying to understand WHAT each item was, there was little point in knowing what the figures were either.

The others listened mainly in silence apart from the odd groan from Gaston as he fiddled with something on his lap.

At the end, finally Madame le Maire gave us a copy of the list she had just read out. If no one else would ask the obvious question I wasn't going to make a fool of myself either. Dirk and I looked at each other.

Madame le Maire distributed more documents that resembled a balance sheet and profit and loss account but not quite, and at this point the Secretary who normally remained silently in the background deftly brought her chair closer to the table. Then Madame le Maire asked for any questions.

A couple of the councillors queried one thing or another and on receiving the glance from Madame le Maire, the Secretary sprang into action.

Quite unlike her usual quiet and demure self, the Secretary seemed possessed, and gave the impression of regarding each innocent question as an assault on her integrity. Two possibilities struck me: either she knew her stuff very thoroughly down to the last centime, or she was defensive because she had about as much grasp of what was going on as I did. I hoped for the former. This was partly because as the Secretary got into full stride, on two occasions the dog joined in as well, yapping with excellent timing as if to emphasise a point.

I thought I ought to contribute something but a voice inside me said, 'Tread very carefully!' I was a bit puzzled as to why we were spending €30,000 repairing the roof of the church. I had understood by this point that the churches in these rural areas are owned by the *commune* which is responsible for structural maintenance, whilst the Church is responsible for internal things like pews. Well not pews, apparently, because we were also spending €892 and 37 centimes on church pews. Ok, I thought, well the Church must be responsible for the maintenance of paintings hanging on the walls. Well not exactly apparently, because there was another item... well you get the gist of it.

Feeling bold, I broke ranks and asked if we could afford €30,000 to repair the roof. This would be a large part of the budget. 'Would it not be a good idea,' I suggested, getting into my flow, 'to have a sinking fund into which we pay the same annual amount which would cover the ups and downs of church costs and make our contributions more uniform each year?'

Now as you might have guessed, by this time my French had deserted me, and I found myself with a raised arm and an index finger sticking out in front of me drawing a graph in the air from my left to right (the wrong way around for everybody else) drawing an imaginary line with peaks and troughs that looked something like a section through the Alps, superimposed by a straight line from left to right.

It was clear from the faces around the table that no one except Dirk had any idea what I was talking about.

I tried a different tack and once again the expression 'digging holes' comes to mind. 'Why,' I asked, 'are we repairing and replacing pictures and pews?'

Dirk rode to the rescue. Prefacing his remarks as always in his diplomatic way with, 'I think what Mike is trying to say is that.....'

He repeated what I had said. At least that is how it sounded to me. Yes, OK, what he said was in fact a translation without the inclusion of my massacring of the French language. Madame le Maire got the point and explained that it was for the benefit of the *commune*.

'Aah, so we can use the church for communal activities, can we?' I asked.

'Yeeees ...' she said guardedly.

'What, like playing bingo?' I returned too cheekily, hoping she would get this point as well. But I think the attack was defeated judging by the bodyless eyes glancing around at the councillors for a hint of recognition that what I had said related to the subject in hand. From the faces around the table no one had any idea what I was talking about except Dirk and even he knew when to draw the line.

'Aaah', she exclaimed, in what I thought might be a recognition of my point but was in fact confirmation in her own mind that either I was talking rubbish or the point I was trying to make was rubbish but either way we could swiftly move on to the next subject.

The dog put its front paws on the table alongside Madame le Maire, looked me and barked a few yaps of solidarity with Madame le Maire as if to say, 'Yes come on, let's move on.'

Towards the end of the budget discussions the floating eyes looked down at what we all had to guess were letters from various individuals or associations requesting money. It goes without saying that they are all good causes, and we had to decide which we thought were the most deserving. Any recipient from a previous year would have a head start already.

Some requests would benefit sectors of the residents, such as a subsidised taxi service to the local town on market day for old people (almost everyone), and some benefited very few, such as a couple who wanted subsidised transport to take their daughter to subsidised piano lessons because they thought she was Gifted.

Dirk and I looked at each other and he was bold enough to make some flippant remark about his own daughters and a contribution towards the swimming pool he was installing, but this did not go down well with Madame le Maire.

The amounts of money being given to these requests was stated to be 20 or 25 or 30 or thereabouts. I said to Dirk I presume we are talking thousands of euros. Just then the Secretary made it clear when reading from the list of previous recipients that we were talking euros only, and that the total budget for these requests was, well there wasn't a budget. If there had been it would be about €250.

One request that raised some comment was a contribution to a Sanctuary providing accommodation for dogs who seemed to have got lost. There was good reason to support this as it happened, because the *commune* was adjacent to the forest and hunters' dogs with no identification were often found by the local people and the Sanctuary was the last Resort. Understandably the Sanctuary had taken the view that if we wanted them to help us we must help them. So, after 10 minutes' discussion it was proposed and agreed that we give them €25.

Once again on cue the dog paused from its activities chewing people's shoes under the table and placing both paws on the table, yapped louder than ever.

This led the voice behind the wall to recount a story where some years previously the voice had been telephoned by one of the inhabitants who had found a dog that was suspected of killing chickens and had now been securely tied to a tree. The Sanctuary were telephoned, and preparations made for delivery of the offending dog two days later.

The rest of that day and most of the evening Madame le Maire looked after the dog whilst telephoning people within the commune to secure suitable transport. At last a small van was offered. Then it was realised that the dog needed a cage otherwise he might run riot in the van. When eventually a suitable cage was found it was discovered on arrival that the available transport was not big enough for the cage. Finally, a van large enough for the cage, dog, driver and passenger was found at the last minute. The cage was secured in the rear of the van, and five minutes and two packets of dog biscuits later, the dog was persuaded to go in the cage for the trip to the sanctuary, two and a half hours away.

After various stops en route, arrival time was a few hours later than had been agreed and the man in charge, a kindly soul, opened the gates to let the van in.

Once in the compound Madame le Maire opened the back doors, grasped the lead with relief and encouraged the dog out of the cage and van. He did not need much encouragement and leapt to the ground, whereupon the temporary chain around his neck came loose. As the van driver handed the lead to the kindly soul, he found himself holding a strip of leather with a chain on the end resting on the ground but alas no dog inside it.

Before the main gates could be closed the dog had escaped and was never seen again.

Having recounted this sad tale, the voice stood up, pushed the chair back, and proceeded to explain to those who could understand French the meaning of the rows and columns on the table on the blackboard. The gist of this was that the budget enabled us to maintain existing tax rates.

Dirk leaned over and said, 'It's all decided before this meeting, you know. We're just here to fill the space.'

As the meeting ended at 00:45, I realised that this was all so much above my head that I would unquestionably return home and agree with my wife how best to extricate myself, because I wasn't doing justice to my electorate and was just making a fool of myself.

It must have been two people's birthdays that day, because quite a lot of sparkling wine came out after the meeting together with some sweet wine, accompanied by lots of cake.

Much later as we all left the Marie I was hoping to find out who the dog belonged to. However, I noticed the dog leave on its own and run down the lane alone.

On arriving home at 02:30 my wife was of course asleep but turned over when I came in, and just looked at me, saying nothing.

I took a deep breath. 'Budget meeting.' I said as firmly as I could. 'Loz of figures, mostly starting with 90 something. I'll get the hang of it. And there was this dog...' my voice trailed off.

'Have you been drinking?' she asked, only half awake.

‘Well it was a long meeting and two people's birthdays,’ I said, grateful for the opportunity of a diversion.

‘Oh, whose?’ she asked, and I realised that once again I hadn’t found out whose birthdays they were.

‘We couldn't just leave the cake. And there was this dog...’ but my voice trailed off as I looked down and saw that she was asleep once again.

CHAPTER 4

AGGRESSIVE INSECTS AND FRENCHMEN

With the approach of summer, I was becoming more relaxed about the meetings. I even ventured a comment or two if I thought no one was listening, but all the words seemed to come out the wrong way if I thought everyone was listening.

In fairness to Madame le Maire, she did her best to help me get my words out, but as I suspect she had no idea what I was trying to say either, all she could do was to hold up both hands in the air when she could see I wanted to say something and say, 'Mike is trying to say something,' and leave me to it. If I was nervous before, then after this introduction I was shaking, but I had been elected and I was determined not to waste the opportunity to stand up for the things I firmly believed in.

Often Dirk would come to my rescue, not only because he is Dutch and therefore fluent in French and English, but because he is a lovely man and not afraid to do the right thing even if it is uncomfortable.

When it came to say my little piece on a subject I usually started with an amalgamation of phrases I had practised earlier. This would invariably produce what one might call a zero response from the others around the table. I was confused if not exasperated, having felt that I had delivered what at the time to me seemed *almost* perfect French, though which I now acknowledge would have been impossible for a native French speaker to make any sense of.

Dirk of course understood not only the two or three words of (poorly pronounced) French but also the several words of Franglais I had used, together with the odd English word. Without wishing to steal my limelight in any way Dirk would, in his smooth manner, preface what he was about to say with, ‘I think what Mike is trying to say is...’, and then he would launch into what seemed to me the very same speech that I had practised so well almost word-for-word the same as mine, and yet which incredibly to me, everyone seemed to understand.

One summer evening as I walked into a meeting I knew straight away that something was up. For one thing, the three ladies at the other end of the table were not in full flow, and they were making furtive glances at the ceiling.

As I came in and took my place at the table, I heard the reason for the glancing and gesturing to the ceiling. The cause was a loud buzz emanating from a huge insect which in the opinion of all was a large hornet. A hornet is larger than a big wasp and a large hornet is enormous, or so it seems when you also know that its venom can kill with one sting.

As the meeting got under way, we caught glimpses of it flying here and there generally clinging to the fluorescent light ceiling fittings which gave it the hope of finding freedom.

Occasionally the buzzing stopped, and we would look up at the ceiling pretending not to be afraid when we located the creature pausing for breath beneath one of the lights and jumping off again when it became too hot.

I however, was not afraid to let everyone know I *was* frightened by the hornet. I suggested to Madame le Maire that I go and open the door and turn on the light outside to encourage the creature to leave and find freedom, and thus safety for us all. However, Madame le Maire did not seem to have the same fear as I did, and she made a series of sounds that I think meant that if left alone it would do us no harm.

The meeting started and for the first half an hour most people's attention focused on the buzzing aloft, and the occasional respite while it rested. As time went on we became less interested in the creature and more focused on what Madame le Maire was trying to say.

For once I thought I knew what the subject of the discussion was, and it was something on which I had a point of view.

Normally there is a sort of subconscious checklist before one says anything in another language to a group of people. This list includes;

Do you understand the subject under discussion?

Do you have something sensible to say?

Do you think you can say it without making a fool of yourself?

Do you think people will understand what you are saying?

Have people stopped talking or are they just pausing for breath?

If the last point is affirmative, have they stopped talking because there is nothing more to say on the subject, or are they waiting for someone else to say something?

Finally, if you can correctly remember the answers to the first on the list you can go ahead and say your piece. Which is exactly what I did on this occasion.

Now usually after I said something they would all look at the one another, hoping to get some explanation of what it was I had said, and would look at me enquiringly hoping for a more informative and understandable way of conveying my thoughts, or as a last resort, they would turn to Dirk for help.

They all remained completely silent and stared at me. The dog included.

Three possibilities crossed my mind:

Either they were in complete agreement with my revolutionary comment and could not understand how they could possibly have failed to come up with the same idea themselves and what a clever chap I was after all,

Or

They had not understood a single word I said, including Dirk and Madame le Maire,

Or lastly

A lot of what I had said or that they *thought* I had said was something terribly wrong and unmentionable in private or public.

After what seemed like a minute but was probably only 10 seconds, Jean-Luc, the very large Frenchman with the strong accent and who is hard of hearing in one ear, pushed back his chair and made to get up.

He had a sterner look on his face than I had ever seen. This was not the expression of a man who is grateful for my brilliant revolutionary comment. His face took on what I can only describe as an angry contortion with slit eyes and furrowed brow as through gritted teeth he issued a grunt accompanied by a gesture I had not seen before.

He stood, slightly bent forward at first, not taking his eyes off me, with his arms straightened in my direction, palms facing up, quite still at first, and then moving his arms up and down as though assessing the weight of a large box.

He stood up to his full height and started to walk around the table towards me. I looked at the others and they all had expressions which I interpreted correctly as fear of what was about to take place. 'No,' I wanted to say, 'you must have all misunderstood. I didn't mean to say anything rude about the French'. But there was no time to work out the translation.

As Jean-Luc got closer I turned towards him, and I could see that his gesture of the hands clearly intended that I should put my arms up to shoulder level in the manner of a boxer. At the same time, he put his own arms up in the same way, drawing them back slightly with his huge shoulders. His hands were now clenched in a tight fist twice the size of mine.

Now I'm not experienced at fighting, but it did occur to me that I would be better off hitting him before he hit me. Nevertheless, I thought appeasement might work, so I started to lower my arms, but he grunted something quickly and motioned me to keep my arms up high. Then before I knew it his right arm went back, his hips swung forward in the manner of a practised fighter, and I prepared myself for the knockout blow.

In a blur I saw his hand coming towards me but to my surprise it was not my face he hit but my armpit. I thought I was in luck, that it was a poor shot. But before I could land a blow on him, he had leapt to my side and was jumping up and down on something on the floor, joined excitedly by the hitherto unnoticed dog who until this moment had, along with all the councillors, simply been staring at me.

Quite oblivious to me but in full view of everyone else, just as I had spoken my piece a few minutes earlier, the hornet had descended and landed on the chest pocket of my shirt before crawling towards my armpit where it had disappeared in the folds of my shirt.

Jean-Luc astutely realised that in the folds of my armpit it was only a matter of time before an inadvertent movement of the upper arm would have squashed the little bugger. But not before he had given me something to remember him by.

When we were quite sure that the hornet had been put to rest I effusively shook hands with my new friend.

With the warm evening and my pleasure at still being alive, the wine flowed freely after the meeting. Someone had just had a birthday, or was it someone else's birthday coming shortly? I wasn't quite sure.

Much later, I crawled into bed and my wife asked how it went. I explained that I had been threatened, attacked, almost knocked out and nearly stung to death but I had come through it. 'Very good,' she said, and fell asleep.

CHAPTER 5

A LITTLE TASK 1

At the start of these meetings Madame le Maire recorded apologies for absence in the normal way and then read out every word of the Minutes of the previous meeting. So that about half an hour after the meeting was due to start we finally got on to the items for discussion at this meeting. Apart from it being time-consuming, it was extremely difficult for me to listen, translate, understand and retain while Madame le Maire continued.

Under ‘Any Other Business’ at the end of the previous meeting, feeling on good form from my near-death escape, I had asked if it would be possible for us to read the Minutes *before* the meeting to give us all a chance to look at them to check if we were happy. This would obviously also save Madame le Maire the time and trouble of reading it all out line by line. My suggestion was met with great suspicion, which if voiced would have sounded something like ‘What do you mean, *check whether you are happy?* What, give people the chance to pick up the nuances and slanted interpretations so that they could be challenged at the next meeting?’

No. Apparently, Madame le Maire could see all sorts of practical and technical reasons why this would be quite impossible. After all, they were only just getting to grips with email.

It was during the next meeting that it dawned on me that various tasks and responsibilities were being allocated to everyone in the room except me. These responsibilities included First Adjoint (sort of deputy to the Maire), and Second Adjoint (a sort of standby deputy in case the first deputy should become incapacitated). These were the two main jobs, highly sought-after because like the Maire's job they carried a salary.

Once these jobs had been allocated there was less enthusiasm for what was left. Generally, as far as I could gather what was left included responsibility for liaison with various statutory Authorities, Utilities and suchlike, all known by inscrutable acronyms seemingly known only to Madame le Maire.

Several times when there were no takers for a role she would cast around the room trying to make eye contact with someone who had not already been allocated something. I noticed that she avoided making eye contact with me.

When a couple of jobs came up and there were no takers, I took the initiative and volunteered myself, having little or no idea what I was offering myself for. Madame le Maire tactfully explained that if I had difficulty grasping the acronym I probably couldn't be relied upon to represent the *commune*'s interest, and that such matters were better left to native French speakers. At least I felt I had made the effort.

It was during this meeting that Madame le Maire took a deep breath and recounted such a tale of woe that we were all incredulous.

'It was 11 years ago,' Madame le Maire declared, 'that documents were submitted to an Englishman by the name of Mr McCloud, owner of a property known as La Boussole, setting out the terms of an exchange of land whereby he was to surrender to the council a small piece of his land (where the council had in fact already located a water pump in an enclosure), and in return the council would surrender to him a slightly larger piece of land by the side of his house on which he could then park his cars.'

It transpired that not only had the water pump been installed and enclosed, but also the other piece of land was clearly already in use by Mr McCloud, 'who not only parked his cars on it but had built a double garage.'

Unfortunately, well actually '*Annoyingly*,' as Madam le Maire explained, 'he has totally ignored, let alone failed to complete the documentation which would legalise the business once and for all.'

As the monologue proceeded, the Maire's outrage was demonstrated by her hands, which once or twice went to touch the stitched edges of the cardigan, until she could resist it no longer and on the third mentioning of him failing to complete documents there was an unstoppable movement of both hands towards the seamed edges which were rapidly drawn tight together.

Madame le Maire suggested that here was a little task I could do tying up the loose ends and getting the documents signed.

I felt a sense of excitement because here was something that I could get my teeth into. It was right up my street.

Firstly, Mr McCloud was British.

Secondly, unknown to everyone else in the room, the notaire involved in preparing the documents was the same one we had used to buy our house, and I knew that she spoke perfect English.

Thirdly, property and land transactions were what I had been involved with all my working life.

Here was my first real chance to make my mark, and the job was handed to me to the great relief of everybody else. The tilted head of Madame le Maire and the deep lines on the forehead told me that

I better not make a mess of it and she didn't expect to wait another 11 years before it was completed.

At the end of the meeting I asked for plans and supporting documents and was treated with the same sort of reaction I would have expected if I had asked for a €10,000 bonus on completion. Some plans were produced, but unfortunately none of them tallied with the others, with red lines enclosing different bits of land on each plan, and no indication of which was the agreed final version. I mentioned this when I was alone with Madame le Maire, who admitted privately that there hadn't actually been an agreed final version.

At the beginning of this meeting, after listening to Madame le Maire once again reading out the Minutes of the last meeting about something I did not fully understand, I had thought again how helpful it would be to have advance sight of the minutes, and I determined to raise the subject of notice again.

So, under 'Any Other Business', I explained that of course I did not wish to challenge Madame le Maire on anything, but simply wished to be able to keep up with what we were talking about since I was a poor Englishman anxious to learn the ways of these kind French people, so I wondered again if consideration might be given etc.

Madame le Maire seemed to soften a little bit, and my attempt at closure with a half gallic shrug seemed to do the trick. She agreed to investigate the possibility of a copy for me only and I could almost hear her adding, 'Providing it's used for information only and not to challenge me on anything'.

Of course, it didn't take the others a minute to think that if I had an advance set of Minutes why shouldn't they?

We persuaded Madame le Maire that circulating the Minutes in advance would save a lot of time and save her having to read it all out.

The next morning when I telephoned the notaire to ask for a copy of the documents which had been submitted 11 years ago I was told there were no documents, because the matter was awaiting agreement by the parties before any documents could be prepared.

I started to feel a little uneasy about my new responsibility and the words 'poisoned chalice' came to mind.

A few weeks later, without any fanfare or mention of it whatsoever, the Minutes of our meeting magically arrived with the agenda before the next meeting.

Later that night I told my wife of my little task.

'Doesn't sound so little,' she said.

'Why not?'

'Well if they haven't actually agreed a document...'

'Oh, that will be OK. I have dealt with these things before.'

'Yes, but this is France.'

'I remember a very similar situation,' I said, and I proceeded

to recount it, but a couple of minutes later when I turned around she was fast asleep.

CHAPTER 6

THE PRESIDENTIAL ELECTION

We were now well into Spring and the main subject of conversation was the forthcoming Presidential election.

We learnt from Madame le Maire that le Mairie was to be the polling station for the *commune* as is often the case in France, and Madame le Maire was looking for 'volunteers' to take up the appropriate posts to ensure that the operation went smoothly on the day. Two teams would be required; one to cover the morning and one for the afternoon. There would be 11 of us. Although Frédèric had some very important business to attend to during the early morning in Paris, he hoped to be able to be with us for the afternoon

Out of just over 120 inhabitants, 84 were eligible to vote. This reflected not so much the age profile (nor those detained at the President's pleasure in an institution of one sort or another), but the high number of non-French residents in the *commune*, who were of course ineligible to vote.

On election day as I arrived at the Mairie car park I could hardly fail to notice the 14 election posters, one for each party, that had been attached to the new crowd-control railings recently erected around the perimeter of the four-car car park. Perhaps a somewhat over-zealous approach, I couldn't help thinking.

Inside though, little had changed. The chairs normally at the front of the table had been moved to the wall to allow access to the fourteen neat piles of manifestos that had been placed along that side of the table, one pile for each of the 14 candidates. This would enable voters to match the party they wanted to vote for with the candidate's name (the only information permitted) on the ballot slip.

On its own, symbolic of its importance and neutrality I thought, at the far end of the table was the voting box. This was a transparent plastic box about the size of two shoe boxes, the bottom hinged and locked. On the top was a flap controlled by a little lever. When the lever was pressed, the flap would open to allow a ballot slip to pass through into the box. At the same time, the small counter on top of the box would click up one number.

It was my very important job to oversee this little box, operating it as described each time one vote was dropped into the box, and calling out to no one in particular '*A voté!*'. At the beginning of the day, the counter of course was at zero, and it was all I could do to stop myself from pushing the little lever to see the number on it change.

Half way down the table on the other side was an important-looking book in which were to be recorded the names of those to whom the ballot papers were given. That is, to those eligible to vote, but only after they had produced adequate identification. But in practice, everyone here knew everyone else, so ID was never requested.

It was a good system designed to ensure that the number of votes cast was the same as the number of signatures in the record book of ballot papers given out.

The voting booth itself had been dusted down, spruced up, and dragged out of its normal resting place in the corner to a more prominent position.

As things got underway it became clear that for many, the actual voting was incidental to the real purpose of the exercise, which was to stay as long as possible chatting to anyone who would listen and generally catch up on the latest gossip.

Everyone seemed to know me and was extremely friendly and although I recognised a few faces, embarrassingly I was at a loss to remember more than a handful of names. However, a nod or shake of the head together with the old half-shrug seemed to get me by.

Of course, some took the voting more seriously than others. For some the secrecy element was not especially important, and they returned from the voting booth brandishing their vote almost challenging others to see where the cross lay before putting it at the last second in its envelope and dropping it into the box. '*A voté!*' I shouted.

For one voter however, secrecy appeared to be paramount. He walked through the door with a determined look which he then immediately changed to a false carefree swagger. As he walked down the side of the table, his eyes were drawn to the pile of manifestos of the party that he was interested in, though he was pretending not to be.

On passing the manifesto pile of interest, his hand swooped down and picked up the top one in a way that almost suggested it was random. He tucked it under his arm and started making his ever-so-casual way towards the booth. Halfway there he stopped as though just realising that the party of his liking would be obvious. So he turned and made his way, almost sauntering, back down the line of manifestos, pausing at another pile and picking one up.

However, realising as he started making his way once again towards the booth that anyone could see through this manoeuvre, he returned along the line a couple more times, collecting a manifesto from every pile in the line.

After spending more time in the booth than anyone else, he emerged triumphantly bearing his voting slip in his right hand above his head. He put it in its little envelope and took the envelope to within a few centimetres of the voting box. Suddenly, he reached over with his left hand and tore it in half, and then in half again, before dropping the bits of the envelope and all the manifestos with a flourish into the bin under the table. Then he strode purposefully out, satisfied that he had made his point. Whatever that was.

On the whole things ran smoothly until the arrival of the widow of the former Maire.

She made her entry thus. On the inside of the door into le Mairie, there were three steps leading up to the room itself. These were negotiated in a quite sprightly fashion by almost all the voters, despite their advancing years. But there was one exception. The widow of the former Maire, accompanied (or should I say, supported) by her middle-aged daughter seemed to want to let no one be in any doubt that she was used to making the sort of significant entrance where she expected to be announced. She paused on each step as though waiting for an usher to call for silence.

After taking two full minutes to negotiate the three steps with much moaning and groaning, she finally made it.

Behind her a little queue of three people had formed. One of these people was a complete stranger to us, but she turned out to be an invigilator for one of the main parties.

I did not know, though I think some of the others were aware, that there was an obligation to provide facilities for the disabled. However, within the confines of the space available this had proved impossible to comply with.

Nevertheless, with a look which said, 'I'm here to make trouble!', the invigilator demanded of Madame le Maire the whereabouts of Madame le Maire. After an exchange of points of view, accompanied by much head-shaking and arm-waving on both sides, the invigilator made notes in an official-looking book.

The dog, who was lying stretched out in the middle of the floor so that everyone had to walk around him, cocked up one ear as this conversation developed. As voices became raised he started barking at the invigilator, whether because the commotion had disturbed his sleep or in support of Madame le Maire it was difficult to say.

I think the gist of the invigilator's parting remark was that we had not heard the end of this. We looked at each other as she left and little was voiced, but the shrugs said it all.

As things turned out I remained in charge of the voting box all day. This was probably because Frédèric was unable to join us after all as he had urgent business to attend to in Paris, though he had asked to be kept informed of what took place.

The system of proxy voting meant that a father or mother would sometimes arrive with their own vote plus three other votes (perhaps including children who may not live in the *commune* at all) giving them almost 5% of the votes eligible to be cast.

As 18:00 approached a few of the voters returned and took places on the chairs by the wall to observe the counting, and chat generally.

Madame le Maire tilted her head and squinted at the clock on the wall. Seeing that it read just after 18:00, she was about to call an end to proceedings when a woman came in who thought the voting went on until 19:00. 'I'm sorry,' said Madame le Maire in the manner of a shopkeeper closing for the day, 'We are closed.' I could almost hear her say, 'We're sold out'.

The number on the counter on top of the ballot box was reading 78. I asked one of the others to count the number of signatures in the book recording the ballet papers handed out. '79,' was the answer.

'There must be some mistake,' I said, 'Count them again.' They were counted again. Still 79. I had forgotten about the paper that was torn up and thrown in the rubbish bin.

'What can we do?' I softly asked a couple of the councillors near me. 'There's a discrepancy now.' One of them leaned over me without saying a word and pressed the lever on top of the voting box. The flap opened briefly and the number on the little counter moved from 78 to 79.

'There, now they are the same.' she said

I looked at her in amazement, speechless.

Madame le Maire ceremoniously produced the key to the voting box. She gave it to a councillor, who took the box from me, turned the key and let the envelopes drop onto the table. We stacked them into groups of 10. Except for the last group of eight. Or was it nine? ....

One at a time the envelopes were passed from the neat piles of 10 to another counsellor who took out the contents, put the envelopes on one side and passed the contents to another councillor who read out what was written on the Ballot paper.

Two more councillors with large ledgers made an entry in their respective ledger each time a name was called.

If a vote had been spoilt it was declared '*null*' and placed on one side by the second councillor. This was the first group. They were not included in the number of votes cast.

Votes declared 'void', such as where nothing had been marked on the Ballot paper, were placed in another pile – the second group. Although these papers did not affect the votes received by any of the candidates, they DID count towards the total number of votes declared cast. (Or the other way around.)

The voter who correctly filled out his ballot paper and put it in the envelope but when taking it out of his pocket inadvertently also enclosed his shopping list (1kg potatoes, bunch of bananas and four oranges) would have found his vote placed in the first group.

When all the members of the public had left, and we had finished clearing up we rewarded ourselves with some bottles of sparkling wine and a few cakes that someone had brought, though I am not sure who.

By the time I got home my wife was in bed. I explained about the discrepancy because it had been on my mind, but I wasn't sure whether I had explained it properly or whether she stayed awake for the whole story. Then she sleepily asked how it had gone.

'Well, it was a lot of work. All that preparation, effort, respect for correct procedure and the counting and recording and sending results. The votes from our *commune* probably won't make any difference anyway.'

'How many were there?'

'Well, after excluding those with shopping lists and such like, 78,' I reflected for a moment, 'or 79,' I added.

'Shopping lists?' she queried.

'I'll tell you later.'

'But our 78 votes...'

'Or 79,' I corrected her.

'Or 79,' she added, 'get put together amongst millions of other votes.'

'That's true, but unless it is a close result we may as well not have bothered.'

'Oh, I wouldn't say that. Our 78...' I looked at her, 'or 79,' she added 'could be crucial.'

'That's what I am saying. Wouldn't it be easier to let the large towns and cities vote, and if it wasn't a close result it wouldn't be necessary for a small *commune* like ours to spend all that time and effort in voting just for 78 votes...' she looked at me, 'or 79?' I added.

'No, I don't think that would work.' I had a sneaky feeling that she was right, but I couldn't quite put my finger on why, when she asked something that had been bothering me all evening.

'What will happen if they find out about the discrepancy?'

'Oh, I don't think it will come to light,' I said with more confidence than I felt.

'Unless one person wins by one vote and they check all the returns to see.'

'That's very unlikely,' I said, getting agitated.

'Well, yes but the margin has to be some number or other, and that number could be one.'

'Did you know,' I said changing the subject, 'that Madame le Maire is given a telephone number to call at the prefecture with the results when she is ready? The prefecture then call her back on the number that they have on record for our Mairie, to prevent people reporting false results from a different number. Also, just in case a villain calls the prefecture from a telephone in the Mairie when Madame le Maire is in a different room, she must give a code number previously sent to her by the prefecture. She carries it on her until the next day to ensure that no-one copies it. Then she has to take all the books and voting slips and envelopes to the police station for them to be kept under lock and key until they're securely transported next day to the prefecture.'

'What, in case they need to check a possible error?' she said.

'Good night dear,' I said.

CHAPTER 7

DIFFICULT OR A PUSHOVER?

One evening I received a telephone call at home from Madame le Maire. 'Councillor Hélène has applied for planning permission for a new house. The planning application will be considered shortly by the Planning Authority, but it's unlikely that they will approve it. The proposed site is on farmland, and unless our Council come all-out in favour with a letter of strong support, the application is doomed to fail.'

'I see.'

'You would be willing to agree to support the application, wouldn't you?' asked Madame le Maire

'Well, where is the house?'

She told me.

'Have we seen the plans?'

'Well no you haven't actually *seen* them.'

'Can we consider the plans when we have our next meeting?'

'No, there isn't time,' she said, 'The council need to write a letter with a date no later than today if they support the application.' Her tone of voice had changed a little from '*nice request*' to '*slightly impatient - don't tell me you want to know the details*'.

'But wouldn't it need a resolution of the council?', I asked.

'Yes,'

'But if it needs to be dated today there isn't time.' I must be overlooking something, I thought, 'Is there?' I added.

Her voice changed from '*slightly impatient*' to '*quite impatient - are you criticizing my authority*'? 'We will just tack it on to Any Other Business of the last meeting,' she said matter of factly, as though this was quite normal. 'Well? Will you support it?'

'Why have... WE', (so as not to sound like an accusation) 'left it till the last minute?' I asked, as mildly as I could. No response.

I decided a change of approach was needed but couldn't think of one. 'Well, what were the plans like?' I asked. 'How big was the house?' Not an unreasonable question surely, I thought.

There was a pause at the other end. Then a sound I took to be one of exasperation. 'Everyone else will agree to support the application,' she said, 'but it's got to be unanimous.'

'*Everyone else will*', I mused. Was it just me being cynical, or might she be using the same expression to everyone?

In other words, I thought, if I hold out and don't agree (which surely would not be unreasonable given the limited information being made available to me – virtually zero) Hélène would most likely lose her chance of the house and I will be forever the one who was responsible - and forget ever asking for help on any matter whatsoever when I need it.

Alternatively, am I being too cynical and bureaucratic – let it go - this is a community – this is the way they do things – would they do anything against their own interests? They all support each other here.

'Look,' I could imagine Madame le Maire saying, 'I am the Maire, *I* decide what happens here, you just rubberstamp what I say. You don't think we invited you, a foreigner, on to the council to object to us following a way of life that has seen us good for longer than you can remember?'

But if I AM just a rubber stamp, why DID they invite me on to the council? Perhaps BECAUSE they thought that I was a rubber stamp? In which case MORE reason to dig in. Or was it? If I am going to show them what I am made of, perhaps it would be better to do it with something less personal. The Planning Authority may refuse consent anyway, in which case to object now would be to become unpopular unnecessarily. Not that I did particularly want to object, I just wanted more information on which to base a decision than Madame le Maire's say-so.

Were we all rubber stamps? Surely not, or what was the point at all? Were the local people allowed to object, but not me, because being an incomer, I was just a rubber stamp - my value to the council being that with me there, they could claim that the committee was all inclusive? Was there an unspoken hierarchy of subjects requiring rubberstamping, with trivia being provided for me to be as difficult as I wanted? Were some issues, which I had thought odd at the time, included in Any Other Business just to enable me to vent my objections?

Was the choice between being thorough, correct and wanting to follow the correct procedure, and knowing when to accept the wisdom of Madame le Maire and be flexible?

Put another way, which would be worse, being seen as difficult, or being seen as a pushover?

While Madame le Maire continued talking, my mind wandered back to the time some months previously when I had wanted to speak to Hélène.

I knew where she was living. She lived with her husband and two children in a farmhouse shared with her parents. A farming family.

The house they now wanted to build was just across the road from the existing farmhouse, which was probably a bit too small for the three generations.

On that occasion I knocked once on the front door of the old farmhouse. The grandmother hobbled to open the door.

'Is your daughter there?' I had asked. She had looked at me as though I had asked a stupid question, before shaking her head.

'Do you know where she is?'

'She is at HER house,' was the reply, as though it was the most obvious thing in the world.

'I thought this WAS her house.'

'Oh no, she lives next door,' and she pointed around the side of the house.

I walked in the direction indicated and found another door that I had not noticed before. When the door was opened, by Hélène, it became clear that they had divided the house internally. I suppose this makes living with parents that much easier.

I decided to be a *pushover.*

CHAPTER 8

A LITTLE TASK 2

I went to see Mr McCloud at La Boussole to see the lie of the land for myself and to understand the land swop from his perspective.

I approached the property along a one-kilometre narrow access road with fields on either side. Then the buildings came into view. The layout resembled a capital 'T', with the access road entering from the left along the horizontal bar at the top of the 'T'.

First on my right was a small house. I understood this to be in separate ownership to Mr. McCloud's house. Next, to my left by the side of the road I could see what I guessed was the pump enclosure (at the top of the 'T').

Directly in front of me on the right-hand side of the horizontal at the top of the 'T' stood a garage.

Just below it on the right-hand side of the vertical of the 'T' was a large property - Mr. McCloud's house.

The two houses faced each other across the vertical of the 'T' which separated them by an area of grass and gravel about five meters wide, extending from the top and sloping to the bottom of the vertical of the 'T'.

The front door of Mr. McCloud's house was in the centre of the elevation facing the vertical of the 'T'. I knocked and introduced myself.

You can imagine my surprise when I was told that Mr McCloud had sold the property some 6 years earlier!

He had sold to a Mr Johnson-Smythe, also British, and this gentleman had then sold it to the present owner - who was also British, fortunately for me (and probably for him).

As I expected, the present owner had no knowledge of any documents, and was grateful for my explanation of the reason for the enclosure and the whirring sound it made from time to time. However, he was a little concerned about his right to use the land on which the garage stood - not to mention the garage itself.

The water pump enclosure could not of course be moved, because it was located at the junction of several pipes beneath the ground at that point, and that ground was owned by this new owner. He naturally thought this ownership clearly gave him a little bit of a whip hand in the negotiations to follow. However, I pointed out that should he use his whip, the cost of demolishing the garage and rebuilding another one elsewhere could be high, and he might find planning permission to do so suddenly difficult to obtain.

With my mind racing ahead and seeing a standoff averted, the next question was the difference in size of the two parcels of land. The pumping enclosure occupied about 1 square metre and the garage - well you know how big a double garage is.

I thought it best to come clean, so I explained the concerns of Madame le Maire and the background with Mr. McCloud who according to Madame le Maire had agreed to everything (well almost everything), and who had now apparently sold the property without mentioning it to Madame le Maire.

Reciprocating in honesty, the new owner explained that there was another matter which concerned him. This was that his garden pathway, from the gravelled area to his front door and then though his garden, was owned by the *commune* with only a right of way in his favour. Its value to the *commune* was that it linked the access road to the woodlands on the other side of the house. The pathway then meandered through the woodland leading to nowhere in particular.

Although there was not much demand at any time for members of the *commune* to go to nowhere in particular, the fact that people COULD do so via his garden path, he saw as a negative point should he wish to sell.

He said he would like to offer a diverted footpath around the perimeter of this garden (down the vertical of the 'T') in exchange for the garden footpath which went past his front door. If this could be arranged, then guess what? He was prepared to be extremely cooperative on the question of the enclosure for the water pump.

This job was taking on a new dimension every minute, and my natural curiosity and earnest desire to see a satisfactory conclusion kept getting derailed by the thought of Madame le Maire's tilted head and furrowed brow with the veiled threat of the cardigan.

The business side dealt with, the new owner was happy to show me around his property, part of which he and his wife were in the process of converting into a gite, as well as making some changes to the outside area; changes which resembled a scene from the garden of 'The Good Life'.

The swimming pool was built on sloping ground and was quite attractive, but the new owner explained that they had a lot of trouble with subsidence. It seemed that, because the retaining wall required at the higher end of the pool had not been constructed on adequate foundations, the present owner had had to import a lot of soil and stones which had been deposited at the end with the retaining wall to help prevent the end from breaking away from the rest of the pool.

We exchanged pleasantries and I drove home. Swirling around in my head was how cooperative the two parties might be, what the merits of their respective cases were, and the bargaining power each had if it came to a stand-off.

Later that night as I climbed into bed, I mentioned to my wife that I had been to see the people up the road on council business in my new role as land exchange advisor. I think she was impressed.

'I think you may have been right,' I said.

'Oh, about what?'

'It may not be quite as easy to tie up as Madame le Maire thinks.'

'Or as easy as you thought, too,' she said.

'Yes, well this is only the start. I'm just piecing the bits together. It will be all right in the end.'

'Oh really, dear?' she said, 'That's nice,' before turning over and falling asleep.

CHAPTER 9

FRENCH KNICKERS

The attention given to Madame le Maire generally ebbed and flowed during meetings, and it was not always possible to follow who was contributing to the topic of discussion. This difficulty was due in part to the constant noise coming from the three ladies at the far end of the table (what DID they talk about?). Gaston, with his hands on his lap under the table and eyes focussed on his hands, rarely took part in discussions. Jacques, I noticed said little but gave the impression of taking everything in even when he was apparently asleep. With the absence of Frédèric, who seemed to have a very busy life in Paris, that left about half a dozen of us to keep things moving and make some decisions.

Almost any subject could be guaranteed to raise passion in the breast of these conscientious French folk.

It was often difficult for me to understand when we had finished the Agenda and had moved on to Any Other Business. In fact, often I only knew that Any Other Business was in progress because someone would go and get some cake and two bottles of sparkling wine in order to be ready as the meeting closed without losing a second of precious time.

Consequently, without being sure when Any Other Business either started or stopped until it was too late, it was difficult to raise matters under Any Other Business. This confirmed my view that it was all part of Madame le Maire's cunning strategy to maintain control.

However, on one or two occasions, more by luck than judgment, I got the timing right, and it was under Any Other Business that I raised the question of - well, the question of ladies' knickers.

Let me explain. The Mairie was a distinctive building, not least because it was the only building for perhaps a kilometre in either direction, and had one of the only two lampposts in the *commune.* (The only other lamp post was at the entrance to the track leading to the house of the former Maire.) Originally the local school, but now with a notice board at the entrance to the (four-car) car park for the Mairie, the French flag - and now (sometimes) the European one - and the word 'Mairie' in large letters (though often partially obscured by climbing roses) next to the door, there could be no doubt about this being the hub of power in the *commune.*

At the rear of le Mairie was a flat – previously used by the headmaster when the building was a school – which was now let out by the council.

As summer approached I saw when I passed le Mairie from time to time that the notice board was used as a clothes post. A clothes line attached to it passed over the car park, and the other end was attached to one of the shutters on le Mairie itself.

I couldn't help noticing that most items on the clothes line were ladies' underwear. I am not saying there weren't any other items of clothing but the variety, colour, size and in some cases what purpose they served would I felt have turned the head of any

Frenchman, and it made me wonder whether the lady occupant of the flat had many visitors.

Morals however, were not my concern. I don't think anyone who knows me would call me prudish, but it did seem to me that the impression we wanted to give to people when they saw le Mairie was, well it wasn't THAT anyway.

I let a couple of meetings go without mentioning it but when I eventually did raise the matter under Any Other Business, Madame le Maire looked at me, apparently waiting for me to re-phrase or to expand on the subject and identify the problem. Even the dog was for once quiet and sat alert with head cocked waiting for a ray of light.

It was delicate I admit, and perhaps a better command of French would have been wiser before raising awkward subjects. Even my pal Dirk was unable to see the problem and therefore couldn't help.

I floundered this way and that, trying to delicately explain what concerned me, but at the same time not wanting to sound too much an uptight Englishman. I wondered if Frédèric might have been able to help if he hadn't missed the train from Paris. Making a mental note to stop digging when the trench is big enough in future, I gave a shrug indicating that we could pass on.

Everyone seemed to look from me to the dog who straightened its head and gave a slightly bored bark, and the meeting continued.

The meeting finished, and a couple of bottles of wine and cake appeared on the table. I couldn't quite make out whose birthday it was.

I think even with a much better command of the language I would still have had difficulty in convincing my French audience what the problem was with the knickers, and I was grateful that no one asked me to expand on the matter after the meeting.

On arriving home late my wife was in bed as usual. She asked me if I had raised anything. I deliberated before replying.

'Ladies' underwear.' I said trying to sound nonchalant. 'Ladies' French underwear. French ladies' underwear. A French lady's underwear.'

She turned her head to look at me, an eyebrow raised.

'All right, you don't have to keep saying it,' she said. 'Which lady's underwear did you raise?'.

I felt this conversation was going the wrong way, especially after a few glasses of wine.

'No, I didn't raise anyone's underwear, but you should see the variety of knickers and stuff.'

'It's a bit late now dear,' she said turning over and falling asleep.

CHAPTER 10

PROMISCUOUS BRITS

After attending several meetings my French vocabulary was improving a little.

I was beginning to learn the trick of not trying to understand every word that is said in a conversation, but to pick out the words I could understand and string them together so that they made sense.

The sort of sense that they made depended hugely of course on how many words I could correctly identify. In a sentence with an 'identify' ratio of nine out of 10, I would have been almost certain to produce a result that bore a good resemblance to the speaker's intention.

An identify ratio of five out of 10 was not a result that it would be terribly wise to rely on greatly, especially if some of the missed words were negatives, which could throw the whole thing out. This ratio would be alright for ordering a beef sandwich – it would not be the end of the world if I ended up with a prawn sandwich – but for a conversation with a surgeon about which leg he thinks should be chopped off, it would be wise to delay surgery until a higher identification ratio could be relied upon.

A ratio of three out of 10 or less was a recipe for disaster - especially if one had a level of confidence that was totally unjustified.

What I would kindly call the *uncertainty* of the three out of 10 ratio was exacerbated if allowance was not made for the appearance of '*faux amis*', which tended to crop up with annoying frequency.

Faux amis are those words which look or sound like English words, and consequently there is a quite reasonable tendency to assume that the meaning is the same.

This can lead at best to some amusing misunderstandings, and at worst some disastrous situations.

A particular memory still burned in my mind, and sometimes in my face. It was shortly after I had been elected, Madame le Maire had made a little speech that seemed to congratulate me and give me a little task.

I was very pleased to be recognised and thought worthy of a job. I tried to make a note of what she said, but I was only able to scribble down a few of what I hoped were the key words of Madame le Maire's little speech to me. Looking back, I can see where I went wrong. Most of the words that I wrote down were those that sounded like English words, because these were naturally easier to identify from the torrent of words from Madame le Maire. At the time, this did not seem at all questionable, in fact it seemed sensible because I thought I could be more certain about noting the RIGHT word as opposed to a similar one. So much so that I mostly wrote down the words in English.

When the dog came around to my side and put his paws up next to me on the table, I took it as an endorsement of my election and the sentiments expressed by Madame le Maire. He barked authoritatively twice, as though daring anyone to disagree.

It was soon the end of the meeting and I'm sure it was someone's birthday, but I really can't remember whose, because the wine was flowing rather quickly and of course there were cakes to eat as well.

On arriving home, I found in my jacket pocket the piece of paper with the words I had written down whilst Madame le Maire was speaking. With my new-found confidence after her glowing speech, I rather hastily looked up a couple of words I did not know and joined them all together in the most obvious way. Everything fitted into place, even if it was a bit bizarre.

Later, as my wife dozed next to me in bed, I nudged her gently and said that Madame le Maire wanted me to do a report.

'What do you mean, a report?' she said, half asleep.

'Well a sort of survey.'

'That's good,' she said, 'What's it about?'

'Well, as far as I can understand it's a sort of survey about the sexual habits of the British living in France.'

Wide awake now, she said, 'What!?'

I read out my English version of what I thought Madame le Maire must have said, with the words from my original list underlined;

'Having assisted at the recent election for someone to undertake this report, I am pleased to say that everyone agreed that Mike would be the most eligible to conduct this survey, and we assume that he is happy to take on this new project for the council.

We have for some time suspected the rampant and often disgusting fantasies of the English while embracing in our commune. In particular we must control affairs with the local people, although they may be charming, and enforce a regime for use of condoms.'

'No, she can't possibly have said that!'

'Well that's how I remember it,' I said.

'We will look at it in the morning dear.'

'OK.... About these fantasies, ...'

'We will look at it in the morning.'

'Yes, but do you...'

'IN THE MORNING!'

The next day we went through the original list word by word, with me trying to remember whether I had written the French word as I heard it from Madame le Maire, or the English equivalent that I had guessed at the time. We cross-referenced English and French dictionaries. It is amazing how many possible versions of the short speech are possible, and how much confusion was caused by the *faux amis*, which seem deliberately to set out to trick the unwary (me).

The most plausible version (I was relieved to find) had nothing to do with fantasies.

We wrote it out so that as my wife sensibly suggested I could go and see Madame le Maire later that day and check whether we were right. We underlined the words on my original list.

'*Having attended (= assisté) the recent election I was pleased that it was not necessary to carry forward (= reporter) votes to a second round. We are grateful that Mike was eligible (= eligible for office), and that he will shortly assume his responsibilities for this new project.*

The commune faces new issues creeping up (= rampant) and we must be imaginative (= fantaisie,) perhaps often sharing a degustation (= tasting) of a glass of wine with our English friends while we embrace them to our commune. We need to keep a check (= control) on local questions (= affaires) affecting the charm of the commune, and Mike will help draw up a programme of building preservation (conservation, not preservatif, which is condom).'

It was still a little strange, but it was something I was not embarrassed to discuss with Madame le Maire, who proved to be most helpful, and we got it sorted out in the end.

As I lay in bed that night with my wife, I laughed over the first script I had prepared, admittedly under the influence of a glass of wine. Or possibly two.

I said, 'We never did discuss those fantasies'.

'What fantasies?' she asked innocently.

'The ones in the script I wrote,' I said.

'But the script was wrong,' she said. 'There were no fantasies!'

'No, but you said that we could discuss it in the morning.'

'Yes, but we now know that there was nothing to discuss.'

'Yes, but...'.

'Good night dear.'

CHAPTER 11

A LITTLE TASK 3

At the next council meeting I could see by the look on the faces of the other councillors that they regarded La Boussole as a sort of test or initiation for me: after all, as far as they could see, all I had had to do was get the owner to sign the documents which Madame le Maire had told everyone were all prepared and ready, and whose finalisation was in fact long overdue.

In the hour or two before going to the meeting I practised some of the phrases I knew I would need, but in the heat of the moment they all got jumbled up and I could tell from the stony silence that there was either disapproval of the lack of progress or lack of understanding of what I was saying. Most likely, a combination of both. Once more Dirk to the rescue. As usual Dirk had grasped my complicated summary, and he proceeded to explain in perfect French what I would have found difficulty explaining succinctly in English.

On hearing that the owner wanted to use the water pump enclosure as a bargaining tool to relocate the track which passed his front door, Madame le Maire launched into a tirade about Mr. McCloud and how he had had the documents for 11 years and all he had to do was sign them.

The cardigan was swiftly and firmly drawn to at some point during her monologue, which was also accompanied by much shuffling of papers and banging them down on the table

The level of complication achieved new heights when I learnt that the land to which the new owner wanted to relocate the footpath round the perimeter of his garden, and which he was prepared to surrender for the purpose in exchange for the track past his front door, was not owned by him at all!

It was apparently part of a roadway (the vertical of the 'T') going absolutely nowhere and whose purpose was apparently to enable large vehicles which had presumably been driven straight down the access road to La Boussole, the facility of turning round to avoid the need to reverse one kilometre back to the main road.

I also learnt that the matter of exchanging land was not a simple as I had naively assumed it would be. Not only was no weight to be given to the relative values of the two pieces of land concerned, but they were each to be measured exactly and a value calculated by reference to an amount per square metre, with that rate being applied to both parcels. The rate per square metre was a government-decided figure that applied throughout the whole of France regardless of whether the land in question was a vitally important right of way and therefore quite valuable, or was in the middle of a field leading to the middle of nowhere, in which case it wasn't.

I tried very hard to find out what the rate per square metre might be, but I was told that it was re-calculated each year and questions would need to be asked of a much higher authority than the *commune* to extract the rate for the current year.

I toyed with the idea of asking whether the rate was the one for the year in which the terms were agreed and documented or was it the one for the year in which the document was legally completed (which of course could be years later and would necessitate the continual updating of the agreed terms).

I decided that this was difficult enough to ask in English without attempting it in French. Certainly not without any practising beforehand.

Not only was it not apparently simply a question of the eleven of us round the table ratifying what I would provisionally agree with the owner and then instructing the *notaire*. That would be too easy. Even assuming there was agreement round the table, a series of documents and forms had to be sent off (in triplicate no doubt) to a much higher authority, explaining the background, and the price that had been agreed and why, so that THEY could decide whether to allow it, in which case the *notaire* could draw up or tear up the papers.

And then there was the question of costs. There was a history. In previous land exchange deals costs were shared equally by the *commune* and the party concerned.

By contrast I had the firm view from the outset that if a house owner wanted a land exchange to move a pathway from his front door to around the perimeter of his garden, he should be the one to pay the council's costs in the matter.

However, in this case it was difficult to say which party wanted the exchange most, and it was all complicated by the trump card that each player thought they had.

We decided the councillors should hold an on-site meeting, so that we could walk past the enclosure of the water pump to the garage, and down the track past the front door, halfway to the middle of nowhere, and then back along the proposed new paths on the perimeter of the garden (the site of the vehicle-turning space), which the occupier erroneously thought he owned.

A date was set for this on-site meeting.

By the time I got home my wife was in bed and very drowsy. I said that my project had been the main item of Any Other Business. I explained the complications of land exchange deals and the mechanism for setting the price by reference to square meterage of the parcels and the problems I had had discussing these difficult concepts in French to an antagonistic assembly of eleven councillors. Well, ten, because Frédèric was stuck in Paris with deadlines to make by midnight.

When I turned around, I was surprised to see that my wife was sound asleep.

CHAPTER 12

OUR DOLMEN

Dolmen; 'A burial chamber constructed of large stones, either underground or covered by a mound, and usually consisting of long transepted corridors (gallery graves) or of a distinct chamber and passage (passage graves). The tombs may date from the 4th millennium.'

I had to look it up. I had heard the word in a few of our meetings, usually under Any Other Business.

Our *commune* had one, apparently. It might be expected that such a special feature would be well-signposted. I had been off to look for it a couple of times, my interest aroused after having been stopped while walking, by some bewildered tourists who had driven around in circles trying to find the dolmen, usually having driven a long distance to see it, and finding only one sign on the approach to the *commune* at a forked junction pointing vaguely in one direction or the other, depending on which way the wind had been blowing.

I too had searched fruitlessly for 'our' dolmen, until I had asked Dirk, who gave me precise directions. I reached the area where Dirk said it was, and the first thing that caught my eye was the dog rolling in the long grass. And then there it was, just beyond the dog.

I had found it at last, I thought, almost hidden away in an obscure gap in a hedge half a kilometre from one of the *commune*'s narrow roads along a rough path alongside a vineyard, but with no signage either to it or about it, so it was understandable that tourists had to ask for help.

So here it was last, I thought again. At least, I guessed that is what these four pieces of stone were. Not massive like Stonehenge but four simple pieces of stone. Three stones stood on their edge in the ground, each of them about one metre high and two metres long, forming three sides of a rectangle but not quite touching each other. The fourth stone was approximately three metres long by two metres wide, and it rested horizontally on the other three, forming a little tunnel. Not especially impressive at all.

Until that is, one thought about the weight of a hand-sized piece of this stone, tiny by comparison, yet only just liftable with two hands. The hardness of the surface and density of these stones would have made cutting or shaping them a daunting task. I thought about the tools that would have been needed to extract, lift, shape, transport, and erect them a long, long time ago. It was only then that the magnitude of the achievement became apparent to me, and I could see why people would want to come and experience it, and how much more there was to know about these amazing prehistoric features. I thought it was a pity that it was so tucked away, with no information about its purpose or how it got here. Whilst I was letting my mind wander, the dog came up to the stones, cocked his leg and urinated over one of the side stones.

From time to time under Any Other Business the question of some signage to the dolmen was raised, but nothing was ever done about it. So we were pleased to hear from Madame le Maire that she had received an offer from someone interested in dolmens throughout Europe, offering to provide some signage by the road at the point where the track led from it to the dolmen. We got the impression, although I was not certain, that we would not have to pay for this signage. Perhaps an EU grant, I thought.

Some of the councillors had reservations though, because the lane was narrow and to avoid congestion there would need to be off-road parking arrangements, road and land ownership modifications, drainage and surfacing works. Nevertheless, the sign itself would be free!

When the question of off-road parking had been aired for ten minutes or so, someone wanted to know whether there would be signage at the dolmen itself as an information point for visitors. It was then that Madame le Maire explained that she had forgotten to mention that the offer of signage also included a large board which could be erected close but not too close to the dolmen with a description of what it was all about.

Everyone seemed to have a point of view on exactly where the board should go so that it would be close enough for people to be able to read it and yet not dominate or obscure the dolmen itself.

When it came to discussion of the logistics of moving the board from the road to the dolmen and the method of erection of the board - well now, this was the sort of thing that farm folk understand, and each councillor wanted to air his or her own thoughts on exactly how it should be done. Even the three ladies at the end of the table paused their conversation to offer their thoughts. So a twenty-minute discussion followed, considering how we would get the board from the road to the site of the dolmen, what tools and machinery we would need to put the supports in the ground, how many people would be needed, and so on.

Someone eventually asked when the board might be expected to arrive. 'It's here already!', said Madame le Maire. The discussion became more animated, but I couldn't help wondering why we were being provided with this board completely free of charge by someone we didn't know.

'Have you approved the wording on the board?' I asked Madame le Maire.

'What do you mean?' she asked.

'Well, did you supply the wording for it, or did they suggest wording and you agreed it?'

'Oh, I don't know what's on it,' she said, adding almost as an afterthought, 'It's in the garage,' as though this information might not have been helpful if mentioned sooner, and suggesting that things had advanced further than had previously been revealed.

There still seemed to be more interest however, in the logistics than in the information on the board.

I seemed to be the only one concerned that we were about to put up a board without knowing what was on it.

Taking the opportunity to visit the outside toilet while the discussion continued, I found the garage key on the same ring as the toilet key and opened the garage door. Inside, I saw a large signboard, about 3 metres by 2 metres.

On it was a picture of a dolmen for sure, but it didn't look like the one I had seen, and I wondered whether I was trying to read it upside down. I switched the light on for a better view and tried to read the wording. After puzzling over it for some seconds, I realised it wasn't in French at all. It was in Spanish. And the dolmen picture was of another dolmen altogether, in southern Spain.

On returning to the meeting I explained what I had found, and Madame le Maire went to her office to look for the paperwork. She found the file and on reading it more thoroughly she confirmed that what was on offer was an information board for a dolmen somewhere in the south of Spain.

In the garage it remains to this day. No one knows quite what to do with it. Perhaps if there is a surge of Spanish tourists it may be discussed again, even though it does not relate to our dolmen.

Why anyone should think that in south-west France we would want a board in Spanish with a description of a dolmen nearly a thousand kilometres away was, and remains, a mystery.

CHAPTER 13

A LITTLE TASK 4

The site meeting started well. The first thing we looked at was the enclosure for the pump. Everyone realised that the owner had them over a barrel. Then we looked at the garage and it did not seem as clear cut as it had at first. Then we walked down the pathway past the front door and through the garden past the house, swimming pool and into the woods towards the middle of nowhere.

On the way back along the pathway which ran just outside the garden, and as we were passing the pool in the garden, we came across a large pile of earth and stones which seemed to have been recently deposited, and which was spilling over the path slightly, and we had to negotiate our way around it. This small detour, of perhaps two or three metres, caused much consternation.

Jacques called us to a halt and asked sternly if anyone knew who was responsible for the pile of soil and stone which encroached over the path.

It seemed obvious anyway, so I had to admit that I thought it was the owner who was responsible, but that he had done it for good reason (to support the pool), and not at all to be difficult. In any case the pathway was only an area of cleared bush with a weedy clay path.

Now Jacques was a farmer and had always been a farmer and farmers don't have the reputation of being hard for nothing. All he said was, 'Ask them to get a bulldozer to move the soil off our path. Then we'll see how difficult they want to be over the enclosure of the pump!' Weighing up the strength of each side was becoming an increasingly complicated affair.

But this was not the end by any means. As we made our way up the roadway that was the vehicle turning area, it was Madame le Maire's turn to stop. She stood still for what seemed like several minutes, gazing across the roadway to the electricity post on the other side, close to the smaller house, and back to the side that we were on, where there was no post.

Walking across to the other side, she observed that the cable made its way down from the top of the post into the ground, then presumably under the gravelled, turning roadway, to reappear adjacent to the (McCloud) house, to rise up the wall and enter the electricity meter box fixed to the wall.

I was slow in understanding the significance of this, but the others weren't. Madame le Maire's face reddened, her eyes widened and then squinted, then she ground her teeth so hard I thought they would come loose.

She explained that someone (obviously in her mind Mr McCloud) had taken it upon himself to divert the electricity cable from its original position suspended above the roadway, spanning the road on its way to the house. Madame le Maire made sure there was no other explanation. Whilst the new position was much more visually attractive - in fact, invisible – that was not her concern. It was beneath the road.

There were just two problems with this brilliant/reckless act, and that was that it was not HIS cable to relocate. Nor HIS road to put it under.

Madame le Maire believed Mr Johnson-Smythe, the owner after Mr McCloud, was also responsible, if not complicit, not least because she had once gone to visit the property and had spotted him raking the gravel towards the edges of the road. I did not quite follow Madame le Maire's reasoning, but she firmly believed that this was damning evidence of his guilt.

She strode purposefully back to the car, slammed the door and screeched off with wheels shooting the gravel in all directions,

As I climbed into bed next to my wife later that night she was already quite drowsy.

I described what had happened, and how the balance of power in the negotiations went one way then another as more details became apparent. I described the look on Madame le Maire 's face.

'Oh dear, dear. You don't think you are making it even more complicated than it is, do you?' she said before falling asleep.

CHAPTER 14

GALETTE DAY

One day, during Any Other Business, being unsure about the current subject under discussion, my mind was wondering when suddenly I heard my name and looked up to find Madame le Maire already squinting at me in anticipation of an unintelligible reply to a question which I tried to make my mind recall.

I thought that for some reason she was asking me where I buy my wine. Bearing in mind that we are in the middle of one of the largest wine growing areas in France and thus surrounded by vineyards that enable many local people to earn a living, I didn't like to say, ‘At the supermarket’. In any case it wouldn't be true, but it is convenient from time to time and the prices are the same as at the vineyards.

Nevertheless, I decided that the diplomatic answer would be one of the local vineyards, which is what I came out with. The one I chose, which produces very good white and sparkling wines with which that I had filled up my car for my daughter’s wedding in the UK, clearly wasn't the right answer. I recalled a previous meeting when a question of car parking had arisen, and Madame le Maire wanted to know what suggestions we had if the Mairie's current car park (four cars) was closed for resurfacing. I had suggested then using the parking of this same vineyard, which happened to be adjacent to the Mairie, and the suggestion was met with a sharp intake of breath through the clenched teeth of Madame le Maire. Dirk later explained to me that the Maire's family and that of this wine maker had a feud about 150 years ago and although no one could remember what the disagreement was it still precluded any cooperation.

It turned out on this occasion that the reason for the question about my wine purchase was apparently because adequate stocks would need to be bought for the forthcoming 'Galette day'.

Galette day can be summarised as a Sunday in spring when most of the people in the *commune* attend a mass in the local church at 11:00 followed by aperitifs, nibbles, lunch including barbecue, and a special cake called a Galette that has hidden inside it a small character from the nativity scene. At least it used to be in earlier times. Now it is represented by a token. The festivities are accompanied by much discussion and possibly singing. The main point, I was told, is to see who will get the token, which is exchanged for a crown. At least it used to be a crown, these days it is a paper hat. The lucky finder puts on the hat, which everyone pretends is a crown (not an oppressive aristocratic crown but a 'three kings of Orient are' crown) and they are the King for the day and have the job of providing the cake next year. Except they don't because the Mairie provide it. And.... Well that was it really. Of course, the real objective was to have a jolly good time.

A date was fixed for about three weeks hence and I found myself volunteering to help with the barbecue. It was agreed that I would go to Jacques' house to help him find and assemble all the barbecue bits which had been taken apart after the last BBQ.

I eventually reached Jacques' house a few minutes after the agreed time. When I say *eventually* this is because Jacques lives almost at the top of a hill with nothing else close by except for one other house. Which is *very* close by - almost adjoining in fact, and I had been unsure about which was Jacques's house.

So, knocking on the door of the first house I was disappointed when it wasn't Jacques who answered the door. I asked if this was Jacques' house. The response was slightly suspicious but mainly puzzled.

'Who?'

'Jacques,' I said. The eyes looked up as if in deep concentration.

I was asked 'Who?' again.

'Jacques!' I said, becoming a little bit irritated by this interrogation. After all, Jacques' presence or otherwise should not be something that needed much thought or conjecture.

'No,' was the answer eventually delivered.

I decided I must have got the wrong hill. I got back in the car and was set to continue along the road but hadn't gone more than 20 meters when in the yard of the adjacent house I could see Jacques just closing the tailgate of his ancient Citroën.

A little surprised I turned into the yard.

I asked why he was here and not waiting at home.

'This is my home,' said Jacques, mystified by my question and putting it down no doubt to this curious Englishman.

'No... it's just that I ....' My voice trailed off. 'Never mind,' I said. 'I've come to help with the barbecue,' I explained in case he had forgotten.

He waved in the general direction of the Citroën. 'It's all done,' he said.

'Ok then,' I said, 'I'll follow you up to the church.'

The church stood at the top of the highest hill around. Adjacent to it was the *salle de fêtes* (the community hall), a recently refurbished building used twice a year by the *commune* for this, Galette day, and another event later in the year, very similar but without the Galette, as far as I could understand.

The boot of the ancient Citroën was vast. From it Jacques produced not only a very large oil-drum-type BBQ but also kindling wood, enough blocks of oak, large and small to cook for the entire *commune* for a week, a chair, a small table, several umbrellas, a large parasol with weighted base, bundles of newspaper, a large bin (for the ashes the next day), implements (tongs, pokers, skewers, scissors, slices and so on), a large pair of oven gloves that had seen better days, a beret, and some matches.

As Jacques carried on setting up between the church entrance and the adjacent entrance to the *salle de fêtes* I offered to help. Although I may have been mistaken I got the impression that he felt this was an important job probably best left to a Frenchman.

People started to arrive just before the church service and although I offered to light the barbecue whilst the service was on, Jacques took the precaution of lighting it himself and told me to make sure it didn't go out. Then he disappeared into the church.

As people came up to say hello before going into the church, none of the men could resist moving things around a little bit on the barbecue, rearranging kindling wood or the lumps of oak here and there. So that without the heat being concentrated for long enough on the individual bits of wood, the fire was not looking very good.

Each time I raised my hand to return a piece of wood to where it had been, the dog which had appeared from nowhere growled at me.

Eventually the barbecue went out.

I looked to my watch. Twenty-five minutes before they come out of church. I went to my car and drove home to get more paper and kindling wood, returned, and started lighting the barbecue all over again.

Jacques was very displeased when he came out of the church to find the barbecue little better than when he had left it. He glared at me as though accusing me of wanton tampering.

With Jacques now back in charge, he needed to reassert his authority, and so rejected any helpful suggestions I tried to make.

When the Toulouse sausage was brought out from the kitchen it seemed about a metre long and was carefully curled around in a spiral on the hot grill.

By now everyone had come out of the church and had succumbed to at least two or three glasses of sparkling wine, white wine, or kir, or all three.

Several men came up to the barbecue and, picking up an implement with a sharp point on the end, proceeded to prick the sausage. I advised them that this was a bad idea because it would let the juices run out, drying out the sausage and thus making it more difficult to cook, but Jacques just laughed and said something quite unintelligible to me.

Jacques was having a chat with some of the other men a metre or two away from the barbecue when I could see was it getting very hot, so I suggested that it might be a good time to turn the sausage over.

'No no no,' he said, 'not yet.' But when only seconds later someone else suggested the same thing he was happy to agree, and they turned the sausage over.

This went on, and with everything I suggested being rejected, I felt a little rejected myself, and was considering wandering away, when I suddenly remembered a gift some friends had given me to thank me for looking after their animals whilst they were in the UK the previous week. Knowing how keen I am on barbecuing, they had given me a chef's apron, oven gloves and, most importantly, a chef's hat, all matching and from Fortnum and Masons. If I was lucky, these would still be in the boot of my car where I had put them after they had given me the present three days earlier.

Now the sausage was being removed from the grill and replaced by another.

I wandered away to my car, opened the boot and yes, the chef's outfit was still there. Carrying the hat, apron and gloves I worked my way unobtrusively through the gathering to the barbecue, where once again some of the men were piercing the valuable juices out of the sausage.

After quickly putting on the apron and hat, I took a deep breath and said authoritatively, 'No don't do that. It spoils the cooking process.' A few heads turned to see who was speaking and when Jacques turned around, his eyes nearly popped out. No one said anything as I quickly walked up to the side of the barbecue while putting on the gloves, and taking firm hold of the large pair of tongs from Jacques I said, 'I think we will turn the sausage over now.'

'Oh. Yes,' I heard from a couple of the men, 'quite right.'

'Good idea,' said another. Everyone backed away as I flipped the sausage over with what I hoped was an impressive flourish, at the same time hoping that it wouldn't fall to the ground and be eaten by the salivating dog, who had suddenly appeared.

As I did so I overheard Jacques say to one of the others, 'Is he a real chef?'

Much later after the starter, the sausage, cheese, desert and more of the above for anyone who was interested, with everyone sitting around long tables engrossed in heated conversations requiring gesticulations and much laughter, I noticed that there was a reshuffling going on and that the counsellors were generally rearranging themselves around Madame le Maire at the end of the table. Dirk motioned me to go over and join them.

Madame le Maire opened her bag and brought out some plans of a building that required our consideration very quickly. It seemed that everyone but me knew which building they were talking about and after 10 minutes the discussion was over and an appropriate couple of paragraphs were added to 'Any Other Business' in the next set of minutes, which arrived two weeks later confirming that the plans were approved unanimously by those present.

Few people seemed interested that a council meeting was taking place in the middle of the afternoon halfway through a *commune* fête day. I suspected they've seen it before and it didn't seem anything out of the ordinary.

Much, much later on Galette day, Madame le Maire cornered me and looked hard at me as she said she understood I had been responsible for the sausage. I tried to assess whether it was a glare or simply a stare and whether it was a question or statement.

If it was an admonishment should I (gallantly of course) implicate Jacques in the cooking of the sausage or should I take responsibility?

'That's right,' I said, waiting for the admonishment.

'Very good,' she said, 'It was cooked just right. Well done.'

I beamed, and she smiled at me.

It was quite late when I left, and I noticed the dog, sprawled out in front of the door, surrounded by bits of chewed sausage. He cocked an ear as I approached and glared at me with his one open eye. I eased the door open gently as far as his body, which he refused to move and as he growled a long low growl I squeezed myself between the door and the doorpost, out into the crisp night air.

I must have left my car in the church car park and got a lift with someone, though I don't remember who, and it was rather late as I opened my front door and crept in.

'I thought you said it was a church service and that you wouldn't be late,' said my wife, dozing in front of the fire.

'Well I was in charge of the barbecue and Madame le Maire complimented me on my cooking,' I explained.

'But you can't cook,' she said.

'I know, but no-one noticed, and I think I got away with it.'

CHAPTER 15

A LITTLE TASK 5

I was not looking forward to the next meeting. My concern was quickly proved to be well-founded. As soon as the Minutes had been approved, Madame le Maire ignored the Agenda and, moving straight to Any Other Business, launched into a vivid description of the horrors that could happen to anyone in the vicinity of La Boussole as result of water on the gravel roadway which could drain through the earth with unimaginable consequences when it reached the electricity cable which had been illegally, unofficially and undoubtedly dangerously and most importantly without application to or consent by Madame le Maire, installed by Mr McCloud, or Mr Johnson-Smythe. Or perhaps both.

I chose the wrong approach when I pointed out that every pavement in the country probably had an electricity cable under it and was subject to the consequences of rain and gravity.

Choosing my words more carefully and with an eye on the cardigan I suggested a solution would be to sell the turning area of roadway to the present owner, thus releasing at a stroke the responsibility should the catastrophe as detailed by Madame le Maire come to pass. The proposal gained acceptance and I immediately began planning my approach to the current owner on the subject.

The rest of the meeting passed uneventfully by comparison with the start, apart from a digression by Madame le Maire, who seemed to have forgotten that we had started with Any Other Business. I winked at Dirk as Madame le Maire once again recounted the danger of electricity cables installed without authority under a roadway. Then, taking a new approach, she asked why British people moved every five years, as if this was the root of all her problems.

While Madame le Maire was speaking, my mind drifted back to three years ago and my meeting with Monsieur Ramel, the father of a local wine grower and probably uncle, brother, or cousin of most of the population of our *commune.*

After I had expressed interest in his work on the history of properties in the *commune* in an attempt to understand some of the background of our own farm house, he went to a table, opened the drawer and produced enough plans and drawings to satisfy a Museum library.

He seemed to know all the drawings by heart and pulled out one which at first sight looked as though it had been discarded because it was entirely covered in diagonal lines in both directions. Closer inspection revealed that this was a plan of the *commune*, and the diagonal lines represented the move of one sort or another by someone from one house to another, usually as a result of a marriage.

Monsieur Ramel explained that it was common for at least three generations to occupy a single house, when the marriage of one of the younger members to a young member of another family resulted in the new married life being pursued in the house of one or the other of them, together with their parents and grandparents.

The way he described it made me think of instant babysitters and saving your money for buying a house of your own. But in these rural areas the reason was more practical in terms of a cohesive family upbringing, and the lack of available resources to buy a home of your own. It wouldn't have been a question of saving money on baby sitters – there was no money for baby sitters, and nowhere to go anyway.

My mind floated back to Madame le Maire's question and I considered for a moment explaining why most young people in the UK jumped on the property ladder as early as possible. Not so much to flee the family nest, but with the expectation that they would make more money by leaping every five years from one property to another with each property increasing in value by more than they would make by putting their money into a safe pension scheme.

Of course, for some, the move to France was only seen as a five-year project. For others, having got to grips with things, they wanted to take on another project in France. Or for some, things had not turned out as planned and five years was the least they could stay so that when returning to the UK it did not seem as though they had made a mistake so much as that (as they would tell their friends) they had creamed off such a profit on the French property that they couldn't wait to return to England and capitalise on it.

The reality is that far from creaming off a profit, for most people achieving a profit on their property after five years would not be possible, except in the case of a major refurbishment, especially with fees and taxes on the purchase price at about 8%.

I was now aware that Madame le Maire wanted to pass on to other topics, and her facial gesture told me that an answer was required. Not having the energy to go through the explanation I tried the raised eyebrows shrug and grunt, which seemed to put my answer beyond comprehension and the issue beyond further question.

The meeting continued. I made a mental note to remember whose birthday it was but try as I might it was forgotten by the time I crawled into bed later.

'How did it go?' my wife asked.

'Well, the deal seemed doomed, but I have rescued it with a cunning proposal.'

She took one look at me to see whether it was worth asking me to expand on the cunning proposal. Whether she decided against it or simply fell asleep I did not know.

CHAPTER 16

A LITTLE TASK 6

By the time the next meeting came around I had met the owner again, agreed the deal, marked out the areas of land and measured them up.

The meeting was opened by Madame le Maire who wanted to draw to everyone's attention the insolence of Mr McCloud and Mr Johnson-Smythe, how the documents had been sent out over 11 years ago and had been totally ignored. Not to mention (though she did) the impending disaster of water striking the electricity cable.

As I started speaking and explaining that I had the owner's agreement, I realised that I should have waited several months at least before reporting this, so that the councillors could fully appreciate my negotiating skills.

In any case however, as Madame le Maire explained, that would no longer be a viable solution and I had been wasting my time because the owner of the smaller adjoining house was now found to have a right of way over the gravel roadway from the top to the bottom of it to a parking area on his own land. Thus with this further complication added, I offered to go and have a meeting with the adjoining owner, determined to try and resolve this issue.

On returning home from the meeting, my wife was anxious to ask how it had all gone and whether everyone had agreed to implement my cunning plan. I tried to explain but must I admit that after a couple of drinks and some cake, the complications of it all made it difficult to get the order of explanation right and after repeating myself, getting the rights of way muddled up and twice asking if I had mentioned the dangerous electricity cable, I was quite relieved when she fell asleep before I could complete my explanation.

The adjoining owners were receptive to my suggestion that the right of way would henceforth be from the owner of the adjoining property rather than the council.

I needn't have wasted my time measuring up the various pieces of land because this was a job which a *geométriste* - a land surveyor - would need to be instructed to deal with.

Several more months later we were at last ready to prepare the documents, subject to including the payment either from the council or from the new owner depending on which party would have the net gain of the amount of land - although the new owner was rather worried just in case the rate was too high, in which case he might have to reconsider his position!

We need not have worried. Far from being several hundred euros per square metre which I had feared, it turned out to be nearer to €1.75 per square metre!

Several months after this, Madame le Maire gave the news under Any Other Business that the documents had finally been completed.

Madame le Maire was extremely sceptical of the council being absolved of responsibility should water touch the electricity cable. She reminded us how Mr McCloud had flagrantly flouted the rules and how he and Mr Johnson-Smythe had held on to the papers for eleven years, not to mention (which she did again) the potential danger of water getting together with electricity cables. The meeting finished at midnight.

When I told my wife later that night, she said, ‘Were they all grateful to you for all your work?’

‘Not really, no one said anything at all.’

‘Well,’ she said ‘that’s not right. I have a good mind to go and tell them.....’

But by now I was very tired. ‘Yes dear, quite right,’ I said as I fell asleep.

CHAPTER 17

DIRK AND GEORGES FEEL THE HEAT

In the centre of the *commune* there is a large triangle of grass. The road through the *commune* is on one side, a small hamlet on another and a farmer's field abuts the third side. It looks very attractive as one approaches the *commune* centre, especially when the grass is cut. This job needs doing frequently, especially in spring and autumn when the grass seems to grow almost overnight.

For many years the grass was cut by one of the (many) older occupants of the hamlet on his ride-on mower. He was of Latin temperament and he liked to do things his own way; he did not have much time for rules and regulations, especially if they smacked of Health and Safety.

As an example of his reckless approach to personal safety, he 'improved' his ride-on mower in the following manner. There was a safety device on it so that the engine would only start if someone was sitting on the seat and would automatically cut out if there was no pressure on the seat. A very sensible precaution against accidental self-mowing. Our friend derided this nannying by the machine, and he fastened the seat down firmly with a bungee rope, so the contacts were permanently joined. This saved all that trouble of switching on the engine after getting off the seat and clearing away debris!

The mower was designed so that the cut grass was deflected downwards by a closed flap to the side of the powerful blades. (If the person was of a tidy disposition a collection box could be attached to the side, which opened the flap. But in our friend's eyes, who needs a grass collection box? All that extra work emptying it! So he never used one.)

The only downside of the clever grass-deflecting mechanism of the mower was that, when the grass was wet, it tended to stick to the underside of the flap. This inevitably blocked up the blade area, and it then had to be cleaned by hand – making it necessary to get off the machine, clean it, and get back on again.

The old boy had an answer this irritation too, of course. He had attached a piece of rope from the grass box mechanism to just below the steering wheel. With a flick of his hand, he could fool the safety mechanism into 'thinking' that a grass collection box was fitted, and it would consequently raise the flap. The result of this ingenious action was that all the grass, together with other detritus such as bits of wood and small stones, would shoot out to the side of the moving mower in a dangerous cascade. This had no effect on our chap, who was just delighted to be able to get the job done quickly. The same could not be said for passing motorists, cyclists and pedestrians who would sometimes complain of being showered with grass and worse.

'I think it's about time,' said Dirk, in his calm matter of fact way under Any Other Business at one meeting, 'that we have a review of the grass cutting arrangements for the centre of the *commune*.'

'The old boy has done it for years, what's the problem?' was the general response.

'He may have done it for years, and all more reason why it is a wonder that no one has been hurt. I looked at his mower the other day and it would not pass a basic safety check, let alone current Health and Safety regulations.'

'Look, we need to have the grass cut often to keep up the appearance of the centre of the *commune.* He does a good job so let's just leave him to it,' was the response again.

'If there were an accident,' said Dirk 'with a passing car or someone with a baby, the people sitting around this table would be responsible. We would not be insured for people working on the council's behalf with equipment that did not meet Health and safety standards.'

'You,' (meaning '*you foreigners*') 'worry too much about Health and Safety.'

Dirk said, 'I have here an *attestation* from our insurance company requiring us to confirm that all the council contractors comply with relevant Health and Safety legislation.'

At the mention of the word '*attestation*', a murmur went around the room. If there is one thing that French people respect it is an *attestation.* This is usually, though not always, an official-looking document with the word 'Attestation' in the heading. It is usually nothing more than a statement of fact. However, French people have found, on any subject ranging from car insurance to health or taxation matters, that failure to provide an Attestation when requested can have dire consequences.

They began to come to terms with the need for change.

'We will have to get someone else to cut the grass regularly to maintain its appearance at the centre of the *commune.*'

'Where are we going to find someone?'

'It won't be easy.'

Then someone started to waver. 'We've not had any problems before.'

Dirk felt strongly on this matter. So strongly in fact that he said, 'I will cut the grass myself until we find someone, and you can be sure that my mower will comply with current Health and Safety.'

Most of the other Councillors thought this was an excessive response. But with an eye on the cakes and wine sitting on the table by the window, one by one they conceded.

'I think we should give Dirk a chance,' said Georges, who was generally very solid.

So, most Saturday mornings thereafter Councillor Dirk could be seen cutting grass on the triangle in the centre of the *commune*.

Being Dutch perhaps, his style was quite a contrast to the old boy's. He didn't own a ride-on mower, so he pushed his hand-mower (although the blades were engine-assisted) up and down in meticulous rows, leaving even stripes of dark and light green. He would always empty the cut grass from the grass collection box carefully into sacks and take them away with him when he had finished the job.

Dirk continued to make a very good job of cutting the grass for about two years, because it was impossible to find someone else suitable to take over and in truth, because he made such a good job of it that we ceased trying very hard.

After a couple of years however the grass on the triangle suddenly started to look very poorly. Rather than enhancing the centre of the *commune*, it was a depressing sight that made it look drab. Questions naturally turned to Dirk at the next meeting.

'I am as mystified as you are,' he replied to one questioner.

'You've got the cutting blades too low for this hot weather,' said one farmer councillor.

'The blades are not sharp enough and are tearing the grass up,' said another.

'Look, it's easy for you to criticise,' said Dirk, 'but I am the one who cuts the grass.' In his straightforward Dutch way, he added, 'I got us all out of difficulty 2 years ago....'

'A difficulty you created!' said someone, followed by murmurs of agreement.

'I have been working hard cutting the grass, maintaining our responsibilities.'

'Do we *have* an obligation to maintain this grass?' someone asked. People looked to Madame le Maire, who seemed to know about these things.

'I will have a look through the old title documents and see if there is actually an obligation.'

'Coming back to the issue of the poor condition of the grass,' said Georges, 'as you know I was a botanist. I will undertake to look into the problem and report at the next meeting.'

At the next meeting, as Madame le Maire closed her book, three people immediately got up and started to look for wine and cake, and the ladies at the end of the table continued talking. Madame le Maire looked around smiling, obviously pleased with the meeting. There hadn't been any actual voting, but there was general acceptance of Madame le Maire's proposals, and as usual we would be able to look at the Minutes to see how we had voted. Georges, Dirk and I looked at each other. We all had points to raise.

'Is this Any Other Business?' I asked. Madame le Maire did not hear me. I said it again, but more loudly, and the Secretary nudged Madame le Maire gently on the arm and pointed in my direction.

Madame le Maire adopted the usual facial expression she reserved for me, with the head tilted to one side and the brow furrowed, as if challenging me to say something that she would not hear or understand. At least she was kind enough to smile.

Realising what I believe was a genuine oversight, Madame le Maire hastily acknowledged that this was, indeed, Any Other Business.

The word crept around the table that this was Any Other Business, and the three people looking for sustenance slunk back to the table with the wine and cake, making a pretence of taking part in the proceedings, though actually being far more concerned with unwrapping the cake and uncorking the wine.

Georges called the councillors to order and asked calmly, 'Have any of you been threatened since the last meeting?' We looked at one another to see if this was a joke. 'I said, have any of you been threatened since the last meeting?' By now, we were all intrigued, and not a little alarmed. No one replied in the affirmative. 'I will take that as a 'No'.'

'A week ago,' he said, 'whilst I was walking along the track by such and such, two large men I knew to be in the employ of Monsieur Renard confidently swaggered towards me and blocked my way.' 'It doesn't do to be upsetting people,' said one of the men.

'Especially with things that don't concern you,' said the other.

Georges was puzzled, and he asked them to explain.

'Weed killer,' said the first.

His friend chimed in, 'What we do on our land is none of your business.'

'And we like to keep it that way.'

'You don't want to go taking things into your own hands. Mind your own business or unpleasant things can happen.' And with that they parted and allowed Georges to go past.

Georges took us back to the earlier meeting when there had been a discussion about the grass triangle.

'I had my suspicions, so I took a sample of grass and sent it off for analysis at a local laboratory. They confirmed the presence of weed killer, which they believe was responsible for the poor condition of the grass.

'On getting these results I went to the grass triangle, reached through the fence separating it from Monsieur Renard's field and took a sample of vegetation from the field. I sent this to the same laboratory. The type of insecticide was identical, and the time of application given the condition of the grass is the same as that of the grass of the triangle.

'I went to see Monsieur Renard on his farm later that day and he denied using this banned insecticide. I then confronted him with the laboratory report, at which he threw me out of the house.

'It was 2 days later that I was waylaid on the pathway.'

As this account continued, it captured the attention of everyone else in the room, including the dog. He was beside himself, being unsure what was going on, but he could sense the tension in the room. He settled his confusion by running frantically between Georges, Dirk, and Madame le Maire, stopping occasionally to bark furiously. This of course only added to the confusion. Half-unwrapped pieces of cake were put down on the table alongside half-opened bottles of wine. Gaston glanced up from fiddling with something on his lap. Even the three ladies subdued their conversation for a few minutes. No one doubted Georges' account and there were lurid descriptions by two of the farmers of what might befall Monsieur Renard.

It struck me that Frédèric's views on all this would be of interest. It was a pity that he was not here, instead of tying up some deal with the government in Paris.

Eventually the commotion came to an end, and Dirk and Georges, both now exonerated from any wrongdoing, were permitted to have cake and wine. The atmosphere remained tense.

At the next meeting under Any Other Business, Madame le Maire had something interesting to say.

'I was looking through old title deed files to see whether there was any OBLIGATION on the council to maintain the grass triangle. As you all know we have understood that this land was in the council's ownership for as long as anyone in the *commune* can remember. So you can imagine my surprise to discover that the land is in fact owned by the local *Département* (the county)!'

So, all these years, the land wasn't even the in the *commune's* ownership. All the costs and effort expended maintaining this little patch of land had not been necessary or appropriate. Over as many years as even the oldest of the inhabitants of the *commune* could recall, while the maintenance improved the appearance of the *commune*, it should never have been authorised. I guessed that this could lead to some embarrassment if anyone asked why council money had been spent in maintaining the grass for so long when it belonged to the *Département*.

Madame le Maire had decided that since this irregular state of affairs had continued during her term of office, she had better do something about it.

'I have contacted the *Département,*' she added, 'and suggested that they should take over the responsibility for maintaining the triangle of grass.'

Needless to say, the huge, bureaucratically-burdened *Département* were not very enthusiastic at the thought of maintaining a tiny patch of grass in the middle of the countryside, in a tiny *commune*. 'They suggested instead a transfer of ownership to the council for a token €1. It would then be our Council's responsibility.' Madame le Maire felt that this would rectify the situation neatly, and it was agreed.

It came as no surprise that Dirk's grass cutting was never directly mentioned again.

That night after the Meeting I discussed these issues with my wife, briefly outlining for her all the events and my concerns.

'Why are you concerned?' she asked.

'Well, for example, Dirk and other people have been cutting the grass for years, when the council did not even own the land!'

'Will he have to repay the money he was paid?'

'Oh no.'

'Will Madame le Maire have to repay the money?'

'Oh no.'

'Well then. Is Dirk still cutting the grass?'

'Oh no. The old boy's son has stepped in, and he has a new mower.'

'Has Georges been threatened again?'

'Oh no, the gendarmes went to have a word with Monsieur Renaud.'

'What are you worried about then?'

'But what about the Minutes?'

'What about them?'

'Everything is in there.'

'What happens to them after your council meeting?'

'Well, I suppose they are filed.'

'Does anyone read them after they are filed?'

'Oh no, I shouldn't think so.'

'Well what are you worried about then?'

'Well, nothing I suppose.'

'Quite. Good night dear.'

'Good night dear.'

And with that, we both fell asleep.

CHAPTER 18

ONE AT A TIME, PLEASE

The *commune* owned several properties which it rented out, and under Any Other Business there would often be complaints or requests from one or other of the occupiers about the structure, decorations or something else, and it almost seemed as though they had a pact that each month at least one of them would write and complain - as though they might lose the right to make future requests if they missed out on a month.

The questions raised were often curious, such as complaints that the windows were too small or the chimney too big. This month we had a plastic shower cubicle that was broken in one of the council's houses. We agreed to dispatch an architect who lived in the *commune* to have a look at it.

We received the architect's written report on the cracked shower cubicle, and it turned out that it was in fact the shower tray which was cracked, and the water was leaking onto the floor below. Instructions were about to be given to the architect to replace the shower when someone asked why it was cracked. The architect was dispatched to find out and asked to report at the next meeting.

The architect's next written report confirmed that the shower was not old and was purchased from a reputable supplier who was able to confirm the strength characteristics of this shower. These amounted to a loading capacity of up to 200kg, well within the needs of most people.

So why did it crack? Was it faulty manufacture or installation, or had it been misused?

The architect asked for a personal meeting with us rather than write his next report. He sat at the side during the early part of the meeting, his hands constantly fiddling with his briefcase or his keys.

When it came to his report we awaited his explanation with interest. The couple who rented the house were, the architect explained, both very large people who, were they to get in the shower at the same time, would undoubtedly exceed the loading tolerance.

'Why,' asked Madame le Maire innocently, 'would they both want to have a shower at the same time, especially given their sizes?'.

Knowing glances were exchanged around the room and throats were cleared.

Recognising what we were obviously thinking, Madame le Maire adjusted the cardigan to a closed position and said some of her stock words to fill the gap – 'Écoute, Bon, Maintenant, Alors.' and so on.

The general mood was that the council should not be responsible for damage caused by such antics in the shower cubicle, but no one wanted to have to say so when the problem related to the SIZE of these two people.

It was left to the architect to draft something suitable.

The response from the couple was delivered for the next meeting. They were horrified that we should have thought such things of them. The architect was summoned once more for an explanation of the apparent conflict.

When he duly appeared at the next meeting, someone asked him why two of them would want to go in the shower at same time.

Apparently, the man had broken his arm, and it was in plaster, so he was unable to wash himself, thus requiring the assistance of his wife - and hence the need for both to be in the cubicle at the same time.

We decided unanimously that these amounted to extenuating circumstances and agreed to replace the shower tray.

CHAPTER 19

FRÉDÈRIC

At the end of each calendar year it is normal for the council (well actually, Madame le Maire), to put together an A4 leaflet. This comprises ten or twelve pages detailing what the taxes have been spent on during the past year, what has been achieved by the Council and what is to come, together with births deaths and marriages, and photographs of buildings such as the church and the Mairie.

So just before Christmas when everyone was present (everyone that is except Frédèric), Madame le Maire suggested that it would be nice to have a photograph of her surrounded by her councillors for the leaflet. Someone came to take the photograph and we all stood around outside the Mairie entrance tying to look relaxed. When it was printed, the photograph was in landscape format, and it spread across two A4 sheets in the leaflet. With ten of us in the photograph we were each quite small on the page.

Madame le Maire decided that it would be unreasonable to exclude Frédèric, even though he had not been able to come to any of the meetings. He was after all a councillor, and it would look odd if his picture was not included. Accordingly, she had asked him to send a picture of himself.

It is true that to have added a picture of Frédèric that was the same size as we were in our joint photograph would have been ridiculous – his head would be barely recognisable! On the other hand, I was amused to see that the picture he did send took up a whole quarter-page, making it look as though Frédèric were the main man and all the other councillors were merely helpers. I'm sure this was not intentional, but I wondered if I was the only one who saw the funny side of it.

At about the same time Madame le Maire announced with great pleasure that she had heard from Frédèric that he was going to be able to come home for a week during December, and although Madame le Maire admitted that at the present time there was nothing we needed to discuss during December, it would nevertheless be nice to arrange a meeting that Frédèric would at last be able to attend. A date just before Christmas was fixed for this next meeting, and for the first time ever there were no items for discussion on the Agenda.

I was looking forward with great interest to meeting this elusive Frédèric whom everyone seemed to hold in great reverence.

On the day of the meeting at least two of the councillors phoned me to make sure I was going so that it would be a full turn-out in honour of Frédèric. I arrived 2 minutes before the meeting was due to start and on entering the room I scanned the faces for one I hadn't seen before. Alas, there was no Frédèric yet. There was a buzz of excitement and I noticed that several of the councillors were wearing smarter clothes than normal, no doubt in honour of Frederic's attendance.

Madame le Maire allowed general chat to go on after the meeting should have started but still there was no Frederic. Since there was nothing on the agenda and nothing to formally discuss, after half an hour we were getting restless and someone suggested we telephone Frédèric to see if perhaps he had got the time of the meeting wrong.

Madame le Maire took it upon herself to phone Frédèric at home, and she did so from her office. She came back to report, ‘Sadly Frédèric has a dose of ‘flu and is confined to bed at home. Regretfully he will not be unable to join us on this occasion and suggested that we continue the meeting without him.’

‘I asked him,’ Madame le Maire continued, ‘if he would be available during the next few days. He explained that he is due in Paris in two days’ time and it will be impossible for him to come to a meeting before he leaves.’

The dog let out a long howl.

It being too early for wine and cakes, the meeting was abandoned.

On my arrival home, my wife was eager to hear all about Frédèric.

My description of events only added to our curiosity about the mysterious Frédèric.

Did he really exist, we wondered? Was it a coincidence that Madame le Maire telephoned from her office, out of hearing from the rest of us? If so, whose was the face on the large photograph? The plot thickened.

CHAPTER 20

CHRISTMAS

It was Christmas once again and the annual ritual of festooning the Mairie entrance with tacky bits and pieces had commenced. A week earlier Madame le Maire had asked who would like to volunteer to give up a Saturday morning before Christmas.

It is similar to manning the lifeboats. Generally, those with children were able to claim immunity from this chore as they had to go shopping for family presents. Those who were quick off the mark with some convincing excuse were let off the hook. Those like me, unable to think quickly (the same ones as always) found ourselves on this cold Saturday morning outside the Mairie, chatting and stamping our feet.

Jacques as usual had been given the job of finding a tree. He was not the sort of farmer to waste money going to a shop to buy a Christmas tree when there was a forest full of them on his doorstep. Anyway, no questions were asked when Jacques turned up in his ancient Citroën with the tree inside. When I say inside, there were at least three meters hanging over the rear tailgate, but I still wondered if the tree would be high enough to be impressive.

I had forgotten to make allowance for the Tardis that was Jaques' Citroën. Jacques hauled the tree out of the car and we all gazed in astonishment at the tree now lying on the ground in front of us, thinking it must surely measure at least twice as long as the inside of Jacques' car.

Jaques thought I was possibly a little stupid. At least I thought he did. I think he thought I was possibly a little stupid because I did not speak French very well. And if I did not speak French very well, he reasoned I may have possibly been a little stupid.

It is understandable that Jacques would think this. Quite possibly anyone he met who did not speak French coherently was quite possibly a little stupid.

I'm not saying I'm not stupid. Just that because I didn't speak French coherently didn't mean that I was quite possibly a little stupid.

He reminds me of the caretaker at my local car service station who came out of the sentry-type box on the forecourt one Saturday afternoon when I was expecting the garage to be open. When he heard me massacring the French language he explained, '*Atelier fermé.*'

I suppose because I did not immediately get back into my car and drive off he repeated once again, '*Atelier fermé.*'

Then a third time with emphasis and a gap between the two words '*ATELIER. FERMÉ.*'

Just to be quite clear, in case I hadn't heard or understood, or perhaps because I did not know what the words meant, he broke up the syllables ' *A. tel. ier. fer. mé!*'. The final syllable being pronounced with triumphal enthusiasm.

Then once more, this time with a great sweep of the arm in the direction of the workshop, '*AT EL I ER FERM É!*' leaving no possibility of lingering doubt that workshop was in fact closed.

The general chatting did not abate (the three ladies were in their element – no doubt the season provided endless subjects for discussion) and there was a general movement in the direction of the storage cupboard from which Jaques took a barrel to hold the tree. Judging by the condition of the barrel, it had been used many times for this purpose and had been converted in such a way as to be ideal for the job.

Several boxes were found and taken outside. In the boxes were trimmings, baubles, fairy lights and extension cables, all of which had seen much better days. They were as tired and well-used as the barrel. There is a limited number of times you can hang up and remove tinsel on an outside Christmas tree without the lengths getting too short to be of much use.

Jacques got his chainsaw out of the car and in no time seemed to have the bottom branches off so that the trunk base would fit the barrel.

By comparison with Jacques' tree-erecting, the pace of tree-festooning activity was very slow because there was no overall direction. Everyone seemed to have their own idea about what it would look like when it was finished and what needed doing, but no-one shared these thoughts with anyone else as far as I could tell. Whilst it was obvious (but not all that obvious - see later) that the tinsel was to be hung on the tree, it wasn't quite as clear for example where the lights were to go.

It seemed to me to be the way of doing things that no one was keen to take control over the activities that others might be involved with. I was struck by the contrast with the UK, where with any joint activity, almost everyone wants to be chief. I suppose the French way was a more egalitarian approach. Each person worked towards what they saw as the final appearance. I suggested to Madame le Maire that she give each person an area of responsibility, but she seemed quite surprised at the thought, as though it was revolutionary in both senses of the word.

It was quite possibly the French Revolution which was behind this French attitude that British people find curious and which French people regard as normal. The French Revolution of which the 1789 riots were the turning point, was a period of social and political upheaval in France. It is a fight that French people still relate to and explains why many take Bastille Day seriously. The Revolution overthrew the monarchy, created a republic and paved the way to give Liberté, Égalité and Fraternité to all.

With Great Britain's Guy Fawkes night by comparison, it is difficult to have much allegiance to one side or the other. It is not only that Guy Fawkes was not a ring leader (he just stayed behind to light the fuses) or that he failed in his attempt to blow up the Houses of Parliament. It is also difficult to relate to the protest against the protestant oppression, and it was after all as long ago as 1605. Guy Fawkes night is now just an excuse for a night out. Bastille Day is so much more than that. It represents changes in social order, law, rights and the political system which are still very much at the heart of French life.

This influences their attitudes and relationships in every area of life - even when putting up Christmas lights.

I just offered my services to anyone who seemed as if they needed help.

One of the ladies suggested I get an extension lead out. I did so and started wrapping the cable around one of the beams in the alcove area adjacent to where Jaques had now erected the tree.

I had just started snaking the extension cable around the beam when Jacques came up and said 'No, no, no, not like that!' He showed me a different beam, which in his mind was much more suitable for the cable treatment. I tried to explain that one of the ladies had asked me to do it that way, but Jacques didn't understand or couldn't hear me or didn't want to understand. I suppose thinking I was possibly a little stupid, he didn't think my comments were worth listening to anyway. He started to explain to me how to connect the two cable extensions together and I think he was a little surprised when this slightly stupid Englishman got the hang of it straight away. I am sure he put this down to his excellent demonstration rather than my quick understanding.

(A few weeks later Jaques overheard me in conversation with another Englishman. He said afterwards, 'You speak English very quickly don't you?' I suppose to him the words all seemed joined up, as indeed French words often did to me. I tried to explain this to Jaques but with limited success due again to my poor command of the French language.)

He was a little annoyed when one of the ladies (who was quite understandably unwilling to climb a ladder) suggested that the top of the tree might need securing to something, as though she were questioning his competence. This would account for why he did not climb the step ladder himself to secure the tree, but just left it for me to do. The ladder was one of those very light and quite high aluminium ones and I'm not keen on going up ladders at the best of times. Jaques got the message and indicated that he would hold the bottom of the ladder, for which I was grateful as it had started sinking into the muddy ground as soon as I got on the first step.

It was my fault of course that the tree wasn't secured properly, and he was giving detailed and loud instructions so that everyone could hear exactly how to secure the top of the tree. It involved reaching as far as I could safely reach without falling off the ladder, and I was grateful that Jacques was holding onto it at the bottom. However, when I just managed to get a hold on the piece of rope to attach the tree, the ladder moved and when I looked down Jacques had let go and had gone off to sort some plugs out.

I came down a few rungs from the top where I felt safer, and thought while I was up there, I would start to arrange the tinsel on the tree. I thought this was a fairly innocuous pursuit, but one of the ladies had very strong ideas about which colour was to go at the top, which in the middle and which at the bottom.

I tidied up the tinsel a bit, re-doing some of what I had done in the last five minutes but with the right colours this time. I then came down and taking the same approach as everyone else (whatever seems right), started to attach some lights where I thought they would look best, just under the gutter. 'No, no, no!' (a phrase I was hearing a lot just now) said one of the councillors, 'It doesn't go there,' as if it was part of a grand plan and how could I possibly not be aware of it?

One of the ladies asked if I would go up the ladder again to retrieve some green tinsel which had impertinently blown into the red colour section. As I was climbing the ladder again, the dog made an appearance. He came straight to my ladder and put his front paws on the third rung. I was unsure about this at first, but I decided he was trying to steady the ladder for me. When I accidentally touched the wrong tinsel he barked three times, which sounded just like, 'no, no, no!'

Each time I asked what I could do to help it seemed I was asked to do something that was later countermanded by someone else.

Taking account of the fact that almost everything I had done had then had to be undone, I decided that I would make more of a contribution by not being there at all.

So I left.

I do not know how long it took them to finish decorating the tree, but the next time I went past the Mairie it was all done, and the lights were on and the tree hadn't blown down and I had no doubt that the same scenario would be replayed next year. (It was.)

CHAPTER 21

THE FLAT

The first floor flat that was above the Marie office was originally accommodation for the headmaster when the building was a school. It was normally let out by the council but was currently vacant, following an unsatisfactory period of occupation by the previous tenant who, he had assured Madame le Maire on taking the tenancy, tried to keep himself to himself. Nevertheless, as soon as word got around that he was living there, he had been the subject of much attention (unwanted on his part, he assured Madame le Maire) by several women. They came around at night apparently and hurled abuse and more solid things at him through the windows. The severity of the attacks escalated, and the building was in a poor condition when he eventually left, suddenly and without any notice.

Various items belonging to the council had been removed during this unfortunate tenancy, and it was decided that a complete refurbishment was needed.

The start of building works for the flat refurbishment had been delayed 2 weeks.

Madame le Maire said, ‘The contractor offers his apologies, but his vehicle is in use elsewhere.’

Jaques immediately seized on this, ‘This is quite unacceptable. The contractor had confirmed a start date and should stick to it.’

Madame le Maire said, ‘I understand that the contractor received a request from a local farmer for the hoisting equipment to help complete works on a barn before the crop was harvested.’

Jacques did a quick U-turn, ‘Well if it's for a farmer obviously they take precedence over everything else. You can tell the contractor that will be quite OK.’

The local architect we had used before did a good job and during the late stages of the refurbishment, the plans that we had all approved were tabled by Madame le Maire to confirm progress to date. Someone suggested that we go and look at it, since it was part of the Mairie building and the entrance was only a few meters away.

When the councillors were asked to approve something, a lot more attention was often paid when it was something that they had some knowledge of, as opposed to something outside their normal area of activity.

Thus, the plans for a new garage could be discussed for hours because everyone understood garages - their appearance and purpose. Whereas a decision on an application for an ‘enclosure for a venturi pipe’ might be considered in just a few minutes because no one wanted to ask what it was.

So, a first-floor flat being something everyone could relate to, Madame le Maire found the keys and we all went around to the flat.

As we went up the steep staircase Madame le Maire cautioned us that the builders had been using scaffolding to access the building because the staircase had been declared unsafe. Several of the stair treads near the top had rotted and were being replaced, and great care should be taken. There were as usual several discussions in progress and some were not paying proper attention.

The dog, who until now had been sleeping, leapt up at this exciting departure from the normal humdrum meetings where we stayed in the one room. Just as we were all negotiating the stairs to the flat, with care because the bannister also was not secured, he bounded past us. One of the women had turned down the staircase to face the woman behind, with whom she was in conversation.

Intent on taking care with the bannister, she made sure all her considerable weight was on her feet. Unfortunately, this was one of the dangerous stair treads. To the sound of splintering wood, and at first in a sort of slow motion, her body started to descend vertically. Then in a sudden movement accompanied by a scream, her right leg disappeared, and her upper body dropped.

As her right leg dangled at upper thigh level through the stair, her left leg rested on top of the stairs, and pointing down the staircase. Three of the men moved to her rescue, one on either side and one on the stair below and tried reaching under her armpits to raise the unfortunate lady once more to her normal height. She was quite wedged in and it took a lot of effort to produce any movement. Someone offered to push her feet from underneath but with consideration for her dignity she screamed that this was unnecessary.

Unfortunately, just when the three men had begun to slowly to raise her, there was more creaking, and the realisation struck that at least one third of her weight was added to that of each of the helpers, causing another of the stair treads to collapse. The helper facing her one step below dropped down also so that only his right leg, waist and upper body were visible while his left leg dangled through the stair. The other two helpers tried to maintain their grasp on the poor woman but there were only two of them and given that their only hold on her was her armpits, she dropped again.

The two councillors where now trapped on their respective stairs facing one another with their two noses almost touching. They were reluctant to try and wriggle out for fear of dropping further.

Madame le Maire took charge and after several minutes under her strict guidance both councillors were restored to their normal height, amazingly without any apparent injury apart a few scratches.

We made our way into the flat. It being evening, there were no workman there, but it was clear that the work was nearing completion.

The flat had an open plan kitchen/dining area with room for a settee, and two bedrooms and a bathroom. Of course, it took nearly an hour to look at the flat, slowed down as the inspection was by reminiscences of how things used to be, such as the only toilet for the former pupils having been the outside one. Night-time excursions to the toilet by the headmaster were not fun, especially in adverse weather.

Apparently, the last headmaster had asked the Maire before the current Madame le Maire several times to consider having an internal bathroom installed. It was the 1980s after all. Each time the request was refused, but as soon as the headmaster left when the school closed, the first thing that the Maire did was to have an internal bathroom installed. (This was the same Maire who was responsible for having the commune's only two lamp posts installed. The road through the *commune* is about six kilometres long, dark and winding, mainly through forest or with hedges either side. He considered that two posts would be adequate. Where would be the most suitable place for two lamp posts? Well, one outside the Marie of course, and the other outside his own house!)

On returning to the council room a discussion lasting forty-five minutes took place. Twenty of those minutes were taken up with discussion about the position of the electrical sockets in the flat. Everyone knows what sockets do and so everyone had a view on where they should go.

We were all experts when it came to plugs in the kitchen/dining area, and we knew from experience exactly where someone would, for example, erect an ironing board, and which way round it would go, and in consequence where a plug socket would be needed for it.

Rather than leave such important matters to the architect, there was much scribbling on the plans as to the exact position for all the plug sockets.

I was chatting a few weeks later to the architect, and I mentioned the changes made on the drawing.

'Oh, I ignored those,' he said, 'It's my job to sort out things like that. I'm the architect.'

'Of course,' I agreed.

CHAPTER 22

WATER? DIRK TURNS UP THE PRESSURE

July is a busy time for farmers. So, when a meeting was called for Saturday morning it wasn't a great surprise that there weren't many councillors present. Six were needed for a quorum. Twenty minutes after Madame le Maire started the meeting at 10 o'clock, the five of us had run out of small talk.

Madame le Maire asked the Secretary to telephone the other councillors to see if any were planning to come to the meeting. Dirk was first on the list.

'Hi Dirk,' said the Secretary, 'are you planning to come to the meeting this morning?'

'I replied to your email and explained that I had another appointment today and won't be able to come.'

'I didn't receive it.'

Clearly surprised that an email should go astray, but giving the Secretary the benefit of the doubt, Dirk said he was sorry, but he was not able to come to the meeting.

Interpreting the intake of breath through the pursed lips of Madame le Maire, the Secretary hurriedly continued, 'Yes, but we are only five here and we need six for a quorum.'

'I understand, but I explained in my email I have another appointment and will be unable to come,' repeated Dirk.

'But we need six in order to vote,' persisted the secretary.

Dirk, aware that the conversation would be on speaker in the council room and could be heard by everyone, weakened a little and said that he would do what he could, but if he COULD come, it would only be for a short time.

The Secretary looked to Madame le Maire to see whether this would be acceptable and got an almost imperceptible nod which meant, 'Ok if that's the best you can do but he knows that I know he is playing with us because he knows we need his vote'.

Ten minutes later Dirk arrived.

After the greetings were made and Dirk had sat down, Madame le Maire, reasserting her authority, explained in one sentence the purpose of the vote. Something to do with the fire brigade and maintenance of water hydrants.

'Can we vote then?' asked Madame le Maire.

The substance of the subject wasn't clear to me (though that was not unusual) and I don't think it was fully clear to the others.

Dirk looked at me. We exchanged a slight smile. Turning to Madame le Maire he said, 'I'm sorry but having just got here I didn't hear the background on this.'

'We haven't discussed any background,' said Madame le Maire slightly tersely. 'There isn't any background, we're just voting on new arrangements.'

'I'm sorry,' said Dirk,' I don't understand. Could you please explain?'

Madame le Maire emitted a small sigh to express her incredulity that she should need to explain the details to something we were voting on. She elaborated a little on the brief information already provided.

'I see,' said Dirk, 'so we are voting to pay future invoices from the water company for maintaining the hydrants used by the fire brigade?'

'Well exactly!' said Madame le Maire, as though it had been obvious all along. Clearly expecting this to be the end of the matter, and so that we knew she thought that, she added, 'Can we vote now?'

'Just one thing,' said Dirk, 'Can we see the contract?'

'What contract?' asked Madame le Maire, her hands drawing the two sides of the cardigan tightly together.

'The contract with the water company.'

'Well there isn't one. Never has been.'

'Well on what basis are they going to send us invoices for maintenance of these hydrants?'

'Well, when they need maintaining they'll maintain them and send us an invoice,' said Madame le Maire as though it shouldn't need explaining. She clearly regretted that Dirk was first on the list that the Secretary had telephoned. and must have been silently cursing the strike by air traffic controllers that had resulted in Frédèric's flight being cancelled the previous evening.

'Well how much will it cost and how often will they send us the invoices?' persisted Dirk, now smelling blood. Whatever an onlooker might have thought, he was far too charming for any of the other councillor to think for a second that he was going to make Madame le Maire pay for interrupting his morning.

'Look,' said Madame le Maire raising her voice, 'It's very simple, the water company will maintain them and send us invoices when necessary. Now can we vote for it?'

'How can we vote for it if we don't know how much it will cost and how often they will send invoices?'

I was quite enjoying this and wanted to help, not because Dirk couldn't handle it but just to let Madame le Maire see that we wouldn't be pushed around, and because I felt that the winning team was evident.

'Who has maintained the hydrants until now?' I asked

After giving me a withering look Madame le Maire said, 'Look this is getting out of hand.'

'Well all right,' I said trying a different tack, 'whose land are they on at the moment and whose responsibility are they?'

There was no answer but there was a whispered discussion between Madame le Maire and the Secretary. 'Sometimes you have to take things on trust,' was the only answer forthcoming.

'Just so that we know,' said Dirk pushing the lance in for a final thrust. 'So, we're voting to pay invoices on the basis that we don't have a contract, we don't know how much the invoices will be for, or how frequent they will be, and we don't know on whose land the hydrants are standing or how maintenance has been done until now?'

'If you wish to put it that way, yes,' said Madame le Maire through pursed lips and gathered cardigan, 'can we vote now?'

The dog, clearly bored with the whole thing and not finding water hydrants at all exciting, gave a bark of solidarity with this suggestion.

The proposal was accepted unanimously, and the meeting broke up shortly afterwards. Without cake or wine!

Believing that I had upset Madame le Maire, I was careful to hang around at the end of the meeting to butter her up a little bit. I had had an idea that I thought would help with this, and which I was keen to see put into practice.

I started by saying how wonderful life was in this rural paradise, unchanged for centuries. 'But it is only by passing down skills and knowledge from one generation to the next that the way of life survives.

'Nevertheless, times are changing and most of the younger people are leaving the area to find better-paid work away from the rural *communes*. It is important to keep a record of the traditional ways for future generations.'

Warming to the idea, Madame le Maire agreed.

'Unless someone is tasked with the job,' I continued, 'I am afraid that it will not get done, and this cherished way of life of the people in the *communes* will be lost and will pass out of the collective memory.'

Pressing my point further, I suggested that she might raise it at the next meeting and try and give the job to someone who could handle it well.

'Quite right,' said she, 'but who could that be?'

'Well,' I said, 'it should be someone older, and with lots of experience.' As I spoke, I was casting my mind over the various councillors and wondering which of them might meet the description.

'How about Jacques?' I offered.

'Oh no!' she retorted immediately.

I was puzzled by this instant rejection of what seemed to me an excellent solution. 'Why not?'

'He's only been in the *commune* since 1965!' she spluttered.

I was completely thrown. If dear old Jacques was a newcomer because he had only been there for just over 40 years, what chance did we stand?

CHAPTER 23

HOUSE WITH A VIEW

Towards the end of one meeting, under Any Other Business, Madame le Maire tabled a letter received from the company responsible for power distribution. The letter outlined an irregularity in the position and spacing of recently erected electricity pylons within the *commune*, and the Maire asked us if we had any comments.

I couldn't see what it had to do with the council, as though we might be in the habit of moving electricity pylons around. But such is the way things are apparently done, to make sure everyone has a say. I think Madame le Maire took the view that if someone was creeping around at night moving power cable pylons we ought to know about it, and that this was our opportunity to be involved.

From the accompanying plan produced by satellite it seemed that on what should have been a long straight line of pylons running through the outer regions of the *commune*, one of the pylons appeared out of alignment with all the others, and the distance from it to the pylons on either side wasn't the same as the regimental spacing of all the others.

This little irregularity was clearly not considered to be of great importance, because Madame le Maire gave me the job of carrying out an investigation.

A couple of days later I drove to the part of the *commune* where the pylons were situated. They were on private land, the owner of which lived in a large rambling house at the end of a very long rough track. When I reached the farm yard in front of the house, on first appearance it needed maintenance and some tender loving care. Here is someone, I thought who is not much interested in looking after his property. However, I had to admit that the working areas around the house were accessible and looked well used. In the neat and spacious garage alongside the house were parked a large Mercedes and a new tractor. I don't what it was exactly, but I began to change my first hasty opinion of the owner. Here I thought was a person who knew and did what he wanted. Nevertheless, I could not picture him creeping out at night and moving electricity cables and pylons around.

As I knocked on the door of the large house with its excellent view of the local countryside, I could see the cables which had been drawn to our attention. It was fortunate, I thought, that the supporting pylon was hidden by a small copse of trees just to the right of the house's main view across the valley.

The owner was very affable and when I showed him the plan, was quite willing to come with me to look at the problem that had been drawn to our attention. We walked down the field towards the electricity cable and as we approached the pylon behind the copse, I could see that the distance to the adjoining pylons was indeed different to all the others. That is, it was longer on the left and shorter on the right.

On reaching the copse I could also see that the pylon behind the copse was out of alignment with all the other pylons. I asked if he could throw any light on this.

He was very and forthcoming and explained that whilst walking his dog a few weeks previously he had noticed an orange cross sprayed in paint on the grass in the middle of his nice view of the valley. Confirming his concerns, he found two other crosses to the left and right some distance away at the edge of his field.

He guessed quite rightly that the crosses marked the position of new pylons to be erected.

He told me quite frankly that he had torn up the orange-painted grass, put it in a plastic bag and taken it to the local DIY store, where he matched up the colour with an aerosol spray paint.

He brought the spray paint home, went down the field, and sprayed a cross on the ground behind the copse as much in line as possible without assistance.

'Shouldn't you have written to the electricity company in the first instance?' I asked.

'What for?' He seemed genuinely surprised.

'Well, to see if they would agree to move the pylon.'

'But they would have said 'no'.'

'Maybe,' I admitted, 'but you MIGHT have got the pylon moved.'

'I DID get the pylon moved,' he said with a shrug.

That shrug again. Always a winner. And I couldn't fault his reasoning.

It was the contractors' job to dig foundations on orange crosses and erect pylons, not to question the location of the orange crosses.

Similarly, it was the job of the cable contractors to join up the pylons which they found on the site, and not to question the position of the pylons.

I thanked him for his cooperation and was just shaking hands when I saw the dog sauntering along the line of the cable, as if looking at it in more detail.

'Ahh,' I said, 'is he yours?'

'No,' he said, 'Never seen that one before.'

I reported all this at the next meeting wondering whether the owner would be admonished or worse for his action. Far from it.

'He was,' Madame le Maire confirmed, 'to be congratulated on an expedient strategy and a successful outcome to a tricky situation and without wasting everyone's time.'

I had to admit to a sneaking and growing admiration for the pragmatism of the French people.

As the meeting closed, it was once again recently someone's birthday, and as cake and wine appeared from nowhere I heard other proud stories about French pragmatism.

When I arrived home, my wife was almost asleep in bed, but she asked how it had gone. I explained about the pylon distances and alignment problem.

'Won't it topple over one day?' she asked.

'Well yes,' I said, 'I suppose it might.'

CHAPTER 24

END OF TERM

Without a clear indication of when Any Other Business was starting and finishing, one could easily miss the chance altogether to raise an issue. It was very frustrating. And it wasn't just me. I knew that Dirk and others had a problem with it also. We did ask Madame le Maire to let us know but she was clearly so weighed down by the pressure of office that she often forgot. I am sure it wasn't that she did not want things to be raised without warning.

When Madame le Maire closed her books, possibly inadvertently signalling the start of Any Other Business, it was as though half the councillors took it as a sign that the meeting had finished and immediately started to busy themselves with wine, cake, plates, opening bottles, getting glasses out and generally chatting about anything they hadn't been chatting about during the meeting.

Usually Dirk and I had something to say or a question to ask, and we were both frustrated trying to make ourselves heard (and in my case understood) over all this activity.

The only person in the room who was not unsure exactly when Any Other Business started was of course Madame le Maire, and it was during Any Other Business on this occasion that she raised, with a slight choke in her voice, the fact that after having served as Maire for two terms of office (12 years plus one-year extension due to a clash with the year of the presidential election) she had decided she had had enough.

The words 'Oh no!' ran around the table, coupled with expressions to the effect of 'No, please stay!'. Even the dog who was lying stretched out on the floor put his front paws over his ears. But Madame le Maire would not be moved, and she said it was time to give way to someone younger and fitter. We looked around the table at each other. Neither young nor fit were adjectives that might describe anyone around the table, and it was obvious to us all that she had set the bar too high.

After some debate Madame le Maire softened a little and said that she might be persuaded to stay on after all, but only as a councillor, and not as Madame le Maire.

Dirk, upfront and straightforward as always, declared it might be a useful opportunity to see who else would be leaving the council, and who would be prepared to stay.

Jacques first. Probably the oldest of the councillors he declared that he felt he had done his stint and that he was now too old to really want to stay on - he wanted to start taking things easier. Since he slept during most of the meetings anyway I wasn't sure what he would gain by giving up official duties, but anyway that was his clear decision.

Next Gaston. When we could attract his attention from his fiddling under the table he said that regrettably now he was far too busy with other things and would not be willing to stand again. 'Oh, what sort of other things?' Dirk asked innocently.

Suddenly, as if on cue, the sound of ringing and chiming came from under the table and he triumphantly brought out into the open the source of his enjoyment during Council meetings: it was his mobile phone, on which he had installed mainly games apps.

Next, the three ladies at the end of the table: one had too much to do looking after a sick mother, the second was probably moving away from the area, and the third found the meetings very tiring, which did not surprise me.

Jean-Luc confirmed that he would soon be moving away to be closer to his family.

One by one Dirk asked the question and one by one they all made it clear that they would not wish to stand for a further term.

The only person that Dirk was unable to ask was Frédèric, who had telephoned earlier to say he would like to have come to the meeting but had to be in Paris early in the morning.

Dirk and I had a quick word after the meeting and agreed that we needed to have a talk.

Because neither of us was a French citizen, we were not eligible to be Maire, but if all the other councillors were not standing for another term, and Madame le Maire herself did not wish to continue in that capacity, then we had to find someone else who would be willing to stand as Maire.

We met a few days later in Dirk's house and discussed a short-list of potential Maires. There was one Frenchman who was a life-long resident, and whom Dirk knew well. We agreed that we should approach him.

We talked to him and I agreed with Dirk that he seemed very suitable for the job. There was clearly no point in discussing this with the other councillors because none were willing to stand for a further term, with the possible exception of Madame le Maire.

After a few weeks, and just before the council election, a meeting was called by Madame le Maire to discuss and finalise those who would be standing for election.

To our astonishment all the usual Councillors were sitting around the table apart from Gaston, Jean-Luc and of course Frédèric. Madame le Maire explained coldly that it had come to her attention that some councillors had been approaching certain people to ascertain their willingness to be councillors and perhaps Maire. It was clear that she was talking about Dirk and me, and we justified our action immediately by saying that apart from Madame le Maire all the other Councillors had said they would not stand.

'In which case,' said Dirk, turning to the other councillors, 'what are you all doing here?'

'Oh no,' said Madame le Maire, 'That was not the case at all. No one said they weren't going to stand except Gaston and Jean-Luc'.

Dirk and I were aghast. We looked at the Councillors sitting around the table and could not believe what we were hearing and seeing.

Dirk swung into action first. 'But I asked you if you were going to stand again, and you all said no.'

'No, no. no,' they replied.

'Yes yes yes,' we said.

Then Dirk put it to each councillor one by one that they had said that they would not stand again and each of them one by one refuted the allegation and said that they had said they were thinking about it. Or some such other excuse.

Not only that, but they all rounded on Dirk and me and we were treated like conspirators and traitors.

To no avail we explained again that we had no choice since Madame le Maire did not wish to be Maire again, that Dirk and I were willing to stand as Councillors but were unable to be Maire because of our nationality, and that therefore all we could do was approach people and see if they wanted to be councillor or Maire.

'What else could we have done?'

Dirk was certainly treated as the leading conspirator and I was made to feel like Brutus having aided and abetted him though possibly out of good intentions, having been led astray by Dirk's evil ways.

Madame le Maire explained, 'If the election is successful I have persuaded one of the Councillors present to stand as Maire.'

Dirk and I were of course pleased but at the same time dumbfounded.

Throughout the period leading up to the election all the councillors continued to treat Dirk and me as traitors, and Dirk suspected that word was being spread around generally that he was not to be trusted, which could not have been further from the truth.

The election took place and all the usual councillors were elected. Dirk just scraped in with enough votes. (Even fewer than Frédèric.) Gaston and Jean-Luc were replaced respectively by one of the villagers whom Madame le Maire had approached and the very person whom Dirk had chosen at the start.

At the first meeting after the election, as soon as the new Madame le Maire had been voted in, Dirk, bold as ever, asked whether anyone had any idea why he should poll substantially fewer votes in this election than in the previous one, when normally one would expect the opposite to be the case because people would be familiar with his good work.

The Councillors looked at each other and no one offered any answer to his question. Being Dutch and very straightforward Dirk went further. 'I think it's because bad things were said about me in the run-up to the election,' he said.

'No. That's nonsense,' was the reply.

The atmosphere in the meetings for the next 3 months was dreadful. Dirk disagreed with nearly everything anybody said, and everyone disagreed with anything either of us said.

However, after about three months Dirk missed a couple of meetings. When he returned a sort of truce was declared and things returned to normal, with the new Madame le Maire being assisted, or should I say guided, by the former Madame le Maire (who, although having relinquished the title, seemed somewhat reluctant to let go).

Vigilant and understanding as ever, the dog soon accepted the change in leadership and lay at the feet of the new Madame le Maire, quiet for most of the time, but with just one ear cocked.

CHAPTER 25

FERME AUBERGE

The atmosphere improved as time went on and Madame le Maire must have been feeling pleased with progress.

To help our team spirit even further, under Any Other Business at the last meeting she proposed that we next meet at a local Ferme Auberge (a rural restaurant run by and on a farm). There were only two restaurants near the village and this one was on the village outskirts in the adjoining forest. I had only heard of it recently and I was curious, so I was pleased at the prospect of experiencing it at first hand.

Madame le Maire suggested that we have our 'Meeting' at the restaurant, so it would not be unreasonable for us to collectively charge the cost of the meal to the local budget. I was a bit unsure about this, because I would not want to have to justify to some of the poorer members of the commune why the councillors were living it up at the local restaurant at their expense, but I decided that as always Madame le Maire knows best in such matters.

A couple of dates were suggested and only one suited everyone; everyone, that is except Frédèric, who no doubt had important government business to deal with that evening. He did say that he would be able to manage the other date, but unfortunately no one else could.

The approach to the farm was down a dusty track to a relatively open area that served as a car park, as well as a graveyard for farm implements long since forgotten and well-camouflaged in the long grass. As someone found out while parking.

The hinges on the ancient gate in the fence surrounding the Ferme Auberge squeaked so loudly that the bell suspended on an adjacent post was rendered unnecessary. Clearly used to the squeaking rather than the bell, a jolly, farming type of young woman appeared from the nearby building without waiting for the bell and came to greet us. She had a pretty face, and a lovely smile, but the thing I really noticed was the size of her biceps, and I immediately privately named her The Weetabix Girl.

She led us through the farmyard to an area where we weaved our way between half a dozen tables haphazardly placed in front of the entrance to the former farm building. The operation was still very much a working farm, and this would explain the number and variety of animals freely roaming around outside and inside the yard, and often disappearing into the building as well.

We were shown by The Weetabix Girl into the restaurant, which was part of the converted old farmhouse. Immediately inside the front door, extending to both the right and left, were two narrow rectangular areas which had probably originally been constructed as a conservatory. Each of these areas was just large enough to contain a long trestle table and about a dozen chairs of assorted styles, and little else.

The wall that would have been the original outside wall of the farmhouse now separated the house and the conservatory and enclosed the rear of the rectangular room. This wall had been demolished to about 50 cm above ground level. On the other side of this remaining low wall, the floor of each of the original reception rooms was about 1m lower than the floor on our side. There appeared to be no light in these reception rooms except the little light that reached them from the windows in the current outside wall.

Straight ahead, between the two reception rooms and at our level, was what I took to be the kitchen, judging by the smoke, steam and swearing which came from within.

While I was taking all this in, and before I had got around to thinking about where to sit, I had to quickly step aside as two small goats came running from the kitchen and out into the yard.

Most of the councillors were already there, seated at the long trestle table with Madame le Maire of course in the middle. I sat down, and a cat immediately jumped on to my lap. Before I could shoo it away, something began rubbing the toes of my shoes.

I looked across the table to catch the eye of the people opposite to let them know it was my toes not the table that they were rubbing, but there was no hint that they knew they were playing footsie. I surreptitiously looked under the tablecloth to find the culprit to be another very young goat.

It wasn't long before drinks appeared, courtesy of the Weetabix Girl, and the atmosphere livened up considerably.

More drinks appeared, and I was beginning to feel quite hungry, but there was still no sign of any food. To inject a formal atmosphere into the proceedings, Madame le Maire tabled several drawings for discussion. Unless I was mistaken they bore a similarity to the drawings produced at the Galette day some weeks before.

Someone asked the Weetabix Girl for a menu and she talked through the dishes that were available that evening. Quickly appreciating that it would be very disruptive for our individual selections to be given verbally whilst the discussion over the plans was taking place, Madame le Maire asked if a written menu could be produced.

The Weetabix Girl went away and came back with more bottles, which did not look like anything like a menu, but no one seemed to mind, and the evening carried on, with the intervals between discussion on the plans getting longer.

At last the Weetabix Girl produced a piece of paper which looked like an old envelope on which had been written the menu for that evening. Just the one piece of paper was apparently all that was available, and she suggested that we each put a cross against our choice.

Unfortunately, I was seated nearest to where she was standing, so she handed me the menu with a pen. I noted from a command by Madame le Maire that a selection of starters would be shared by everyone and I glanced quickly at the two columns of main courses that had been written on the rear of the envelope. Not wishing to be seen to be holding things up, I quickly put a cross against my choice and passed the envelope and pen to my neighbour, who did likewise.

It really wasn't a very difficult decision, with only three items on each of the two lists on the envelope, but it is interesting how much consideration some people need to give where food is concerned. There seemed to be endless discussion about which cuts of meat they referred to, how they would be cooked and for how long, and so on. I just got more and more hungry.

Some twenty minutes later the Weetabix Girl reappeared, whisked up the menu and was off to the kitchen.

Next the starters arrived and were surprisingly good - or was I just hungry?

The sounds coming from the kitchen became more urgent now, with pans being scraped, banged, sworn at and rattled. As we were working our way through the mixed starters I did begin to wonder whether I could manage a big main course as well. No doubt sensing that I was filling up, another cat came out of the kitchen and jumped up on my lap.

It seems that the family running the farm really were very kind to their animals, looking after them with great care, even though the family understood that finally they would slaughter the animals which would then be used in the restaurant. This was a natural way of life to them and their animals are a lot better cared for than many others.

The restaurant was a relatively recent venture and the owners had done their best with what was obviously a difficult building to convert. The toilets were situated at the other end of the house, on the lower level of the reception rooms. Visiting them was a major exercise which involved climbing over the half-demolished wall at the rear of the former conservatory and down a small ladder on the other side, taking care to remember to pick up the torch thoughtfully provided on a small table next to the bottom of the ladder. The torch was necessary for locating the toilets, which were at the other end of the house. They were in a vast room which contained nothing but a toilet, a wash basin and a huge old-fashioned pedal-powered sewing machine. It was wise to allow at least ten minutes for this excursion.

The arrival on the scene of the owner (a small man with a balding head, a prominent nose, piercing eyes and an incongruous large black moustache) required immediate attention as he strode purposefully straight from the kitchen, wiping his dirty hands on a clean tea towel hanging from his chef's apron. He took little time in assessing the assembled group. He astutely identified Madame le Maire as being the most important, and rather bizarrely regaled her by reciting from memory a poem, which he followed with a brief history of the farm and more recently the restaurant.

It was clear that he had been sampling some of the wine, and I wondered if he would remember in time that he was supposed to be cooking the meal for us. Finally, he apologised, not for the intrusion, but for having to leave us so that he could get on with the cooking.

About ten minutes later there must have been a lull in preparations in the kitchen because he appeared once more, this time wearing a belt from which hung a very long sword which, because of his slight stature, scraped along the ground as he once again strode purposefully towards us from the kitchen. He addressed everyone this time, and after a short preamble he demonstrated his prowess with the sword.

I wondered if this was a veiled threat to give the restaurant a good review but no, apparently, he was just re-living for our benefit, or perhaps his own, his former mastery with the sword by enacting some of the highlights of his escapades in the army. He then shouted a word of command, sheathed his blade and returned to the kitchen.

He appeared one last time before the food arrived, this time without the sword thankfully. He made his way directly to the wall at the far end. Two screws were fixed to the wall, and on them rested a very large shotgun which, after some unintelligible introduction, he waved around as he described more of his battles. By this time, rivers of sweat were running unhindered down his face and neck and onto his chest. Together with the expression on his face, this created a fierce impression to say the least. Finally, and without explanation, he replaced the shotgun and retired to the kitchen, presumably to sample more wine.

After what seemed an eternity, preceded by much banging, clattering, and swearing in the kitchen, the owner reappeared once again, triumphantly bearing on each spread-out hand above his shoulder a steaming plate.

'Chicken fricassée,' he shouted proudly.

Silence fell, and consternation and discomfort rose. The owner's giant eyebrows and forehead joined together in a common set of horizontal lines with squiggles in them. No one laid a claim on a chicken fricassée.

'This is impossible,' he said, or words to that effect. 'I have another seven of these in the kitchen ready to come out.'

Cleverly realising that there must be some misunderstanding, Madame le Maire immediately took control and, to set an example, said to the owner, 'Alright, give it to me - I'll have a chicken fricassée.'

Someone else said the same to support Madame le Maire, followed by another, and the owner beamed, retreating with honour back to his kitchen, to return shortly with more chicken fricassees.

I think everyone was grateful that the misunderstanding had been resolved without recourse to the sword. Or the shotgun.

Finally, when everyone else has been given a chicken fricassée and I was the last one to be served (being I supposed the least important), the owner leaned across the table and proudly put in front of me a plate with a giant steak on it. Everyone looked at me enviously.

Madame le Maire asked how this could possibly have happened. I think the owner wanted to know as well and called over the Weetabix Girl. It occurred to me at this point that a physical scrap to settle the misunderstanding between the sword-fighting owner, the muscly Weetabix girl and the cunning Madame le Maire would prove interesting. But it was not to come to this, as the Weetabix Girl produced the menu with its two lists side by side.

At the head of the left-hand list was 'Steak' and at the top of the right-hand list 'Chicken Fricassée' and in between the two were 9 crosses, with a last cross to the left of the word 'Steak'.

By now it was clear that all my colleagues had wanted steak.

The explanation that the owner came up with seemed very plausible;

Someone must have wanted chicken fricassée and put a cross to the left of 'chicken fricassée'.

The next wanted steak and so put a cross to the right of the word 'steak'

And so on, until there was no more room, and the last person put a cross on the left side of 'steak'. Madame le Maire let out one of her 'Ahhh!' sounds and decided to put the owner's theory to the test.

'In that case who *did* order the chicken fricassée?' she asked.

Feeling like a naughty school boy I raised my hand, thus admitting my unintentional role as the main culprit in the proceedings.

This brought me such a scowl from Madame le Maire that I wondered if I would ever be allowed back on the council. I was saved from further interrogation however, because at this moment the dog chose to make his first appearance of the evening. He looked up at me, barking, with his head inclined, momentarily bearing a brief resemblance to someone else I knew. I kept my eyes down and did my best to eat the offending steak, hoping to avoid further interrogation. After a few minutes I paused for a moment, putting down my knife and fork.

Madame le Maire reached across the table towards my part-eaten steak. 'Have you finished with it?' she asked, and, not waiting for an answer, she scooped it up in her hand and threw it to the dog. He caught it expertly, and triumphantly took it off to the corner, pausing only to growl a deep low growl when I turned to watch.

A minute later a young man carrying a dog lead in one hand came through the open door and was greeted by a cheer from everyone in the room. Satisfying himself that the dog was alright he made his way round table embracing and shaking hands with everyone. It was not a face I had seen before and I was intrigued to find out who it was.

When he got to me he said, 'Hello you must be Mike. I'm …', but just then there was the sound of a crash of crockery in the kitchen so that I didn't catch his name. He sat down at the other end of the table, ordered some food and made himself at home.

When it was time to go, he put the lead on the dog and went back to his car in the carpark, so I never did find out who it was.

When I returned home my wife was in bed. 'How did it go?' she asked sleepily.

'Well …' I answered,' I think I upset Madame le Maire.'.

'How?'

'Well you see, I wanted chicken and everyone else wanted steak, but I got steak, or at least the dog did, and everyone else got the chicken, and anyway I couldn't argue because there was this man with a sword and gun reciting poetry…'

'How much have you had to drink?' she asked.

I took a deep breath, trying to speak clearly and slowly. 'Just a little. It was strange, someone turned up that I had not seen before, I think it was the dog's mystery owner.'

'Oh, you know who that was,' she said.

'No why, do you?'

'Oh yes. I met his mother in the village today. She said he might be able to join you later.'

'Well who was it?'

'That was Frédèric.'

With which blinding revelation she promptly fell asleep.

36388851R00081

Printed in Great Britain
by Amazon